Biblioasis International Translation Series
General Editor: Stephen Henighan

1. *I Wrote Stone: The Selected Poetry of Ryszard Kapuściński* (Poland)
Translated by Diana Kuprel and Marek Kusiba

2. *Good Morning Comrades*
by Ondjaki (Angola)
Translated by Stephen Henighan

3. *Kahn & Engelmann*
by Hans Eichner (Austria-Canada)
Translated by Jean M. Snook

4. *Dance with Snakes*
by Horacio Castellanos Moya (El Salvador)
Translated by Lee Paula Springer

5. *Black Alley*
by Mauricio Segura (Quebec)
Translated by Dawn M. Cornelio

6. *The Accident*
by Mihail Sebastian (Romania)
Translated by Stephen Henighan

7. *Love Poems*
by Jaime Sabines (Mexico)
Translated by Colin Carberry

8. *The End of the Story*
by Liliana Heker (Argentina)
Translated by Andrea G. Labinger

9. *The Tuner of Silences*
by Mia Couto (Mozambique)
Translated by David Brookshaw

10. *For as Far as the Eye Can See*
by Robert Melançon (Quebec)
Translated by Judith Cowan

11. *Eucalyptus*
by Mauricio Segura (Quebec)
Translated by Donald Winkler

12. *Granma Nineteen and the Soviet's Secret*
by Ondjaki (Angola)
Translated by Stephen Henighan

13. *Montreal Before Spring*
by Robert Melançon (Quebec)
Translated by Donald McGrath

14. *Pensativities: Essays and Provocations*
by Mia Couto (Mozambique)
Translated by David Brookshaw

15. *Arvida*
by Samuel Archibald (Quebec)
Translated by Donald Winkler

16. *The Orange Grove*
by Larry Tremblay (Quebec)
Translated by Sheila Fischman

17. *The Party Wall*
by Catherine Leroux (Quebec)
Translated by Lazer Lederhendler

18. *Black Bread*
by Emili Teixidor (Catalonia)
Translated by Peter Bush

19. *Boundary*
by Andrée A. Michaud (Quebec)
Translated by Donald Winkler

20. *Red, Yellow, Green*
by Alejandro Saravia (Bolivia-Canada)
Translated by María José Giménez

21. *Bookshops: A Reader's History*
by Jorge Carrión (Spain)
Translated by Peter Bush

22. *Transparent City*
by Ondjaki (Angola)
Translated by Stephen Henighan

23. *Oscar*
by Mauricio Segura (Quebec)
Translated by Donald Winkler

24. *Madame Victoria*
by Catherine Leroux (Quebec)
Translated by Lazer Lederhendler

MADAME VICTORIA

CATHERINE LEROUX

Madame Victoria

VARIATIONS

Translated from the French by
Lazer Lederhendler

BIBLIOASIS
WINDSOR, ONTARIO

First published in French by Éditions Alto, Quebec City, 2015.

FIRST EDITION

Library and Archives Canada Cataloguing in Publication

Leroux, Catherine, 1979-
[Madame Victoria. English]
Madame Victoria / Catherine Leroux ; translated from the French by Lazer Lederhendler.

(Biblioasis international translation series ; no. 24)
Translation of French book with same title.
Issued in print and electronic formats.
ISBN 978-1-77196-207-0 (softcover).--ISBN 978-1-77196-208-7 (ebook)

I. Lederhendler, Lazer, 1950-, translator II. Title. III. Title: Madame Victoria. English. IV. Series: Biblioasis international translation series ; no. 24

PS8623.E685M3213 2018 C843'.6 C2018-901732-5
C2018-901733-3

Edited by Stephen Henighan
Copy-edited by Cat London
Cover designed by Natalie Olsen
Typeset by Chris Andrechek

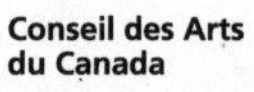

Canadä

Published with the generous assistance of the Canada Council for the Arts, which last year invested $153 million to bring the arts to Canadians throughout the country. Biblioasis also acknowledges the support of the Ontario Arts Council (OAC), an agency of the Government of Ontario, which last year funded 1,709 individual artists and 1,078 organizations in 204 communities across Ontario, for a total of $52.1 million, and the contribution of the Government of Ontario through the Ontario Book Publishing Tax Credit and the Ontario Media Development Corporation. Biblioasis also acknowledges the financial support of the Government of Canada through the National Translation Program for Book Publishing, an initiative of the *Roadmap for Canada's Official Languages 2013–2018: Education, Immigration, Communities*, for our translation activities.

PRINTED AND BOUND IN CANADA

For LFDMV

There ain't no grave
Can hold my body down
—Johnny Cash

GERMAIN LÉON is not fond of the dead. Even though, in comparison with the living, the dead are not much trouble, especially those whose days are numbered, who teeter on the edge of the steep slope that will send them back to the inert matter from which they had emerged. On their deathbeds humans are big babies, incapable of the most basic actions, forced to turn to others—sometimes the love of their life, sometimes a stranger—for their essential needs. These ones Germain is able to love and to care for: wash their withered bodies in lukewarm water, soothe their lips with a sponge, change their bandages and diapers, adjust their pillows, inject with the drug that will make their pain tolerable, then imperceptible. When he does these things Germain is happy; he receives their sighs of relief like little puffs of humanity that make him the person he likes to be, the father he wants to go on being for his daughter.

And yet, while nothing else disgusts him, neither blood nor gangrene nor shit nor vomit, Germain can hardly bear the sight of a corpse. The moment a body has breathed its last, he can't help recoiling to fight back the nausea. After that, like any nurse, he does what needs to be done, but with shivers of revulsion that he must quell on the way home, where his Clara is sitting at the table with her arithmetic exercise books.

Hence his astonishment at the skull. For two full minutes Germain stays frozen, hypnotized by the object that has ended up, God knows how, propped against a curbstone a few metres from his car in the parking lot. He contemplates the sutures that form meandering rivers between the bony plates, thinks of the most famous line in Western theatre, and he marvels at not feeling any fear, aversion, or impulse to bolt in face of this corpse—worse, this fragment of a corpse. For Germain, this represents a surprising new variation among the manifold feelings and impressions collected by people who work in close contact with life, death, and disease. Only the recently deceased disturb him; the ones so long dead that nothing remains but a skeleton leave him unaffected. "So I could go visit Pompeii," he muses before rousing from his reverie.

The police set up a security perimeter around the wooded knoll overlooking the parking lot. Germain tries to see what is going on among the trees, powerless to move away from the skull lying there in the middle of the commotion. He would like to seize the poor dirt-smudged head, to press it to his chest and speak to it softly. He can't explain why, but this bone is the saddest thing he has ever encountered in his twenty-year career. It's almost the solstice, the daylight lingers, and Germain's ears are full of the city's noise, horns and sirens, construction machinery, festivals clamouring away: the grinding works of Montreal. Ordinarily, such sounds are muffled at the Royal Victoria, the hospital so snugly nestled in the fabric of the mountain. But tonight they are amplified, as if the whole city wants to signal the permanent state of emergency in which it lives, the rages, the races, the victories, all that keeps it from sleeping.

Two police come back down the knoll yelling something Germain can't quite make out. They're immediately surrounded by a dozen officers, who are soon joined by the onlookers thronged around the perimeter. Germain hangs back, anxious for no special reason. A female colleague steps out of the crowd and approaches him. "They've found the rest of the body. It has hospital clothes on."

Along with the general public, Germain learns everything else from the newspapers. The skeleton discovered in the woods was two years old. No one has come forward to claim the remains. According to the hospital management, every member of the staff has been accounted for. For weeks, this is all people talk about. During their breaks, orderlies recall former patients who left their beds without telling anyone, and secretaries search through the files to verify their colleagues' theories. Even the anaesthetists deign to put in their two cents worth.

As for Germain, despite being questioned four times a day, he is as clueless as the rest. But he is haunted by his memory of the skull, curses himself for having been so quick to alert the police, like a mother who let her child leave home without taking the time to hug her and whisper the loving words you need to go out into the world. The one they've dubbed Madame Victoria died alone, without the compassionate hands of someone like Germain to accompany her to the final threshold, with no one to mourn her passing. This was the immeasurable sadness he felt on discovering the skull. The weight of that absolute solitude.

The investigation has stalled. The case has been assigned to a forensic anthropologist and crime novel celebrity, who runs new tests on the skeleton and finds that Madame Victoria was a Caucasian women of about fifty suffering from osteoporosis and arthritis-ridden joints but showing no signs of a violent death. Although the conclusions don't rule out murder by poisoning or strangulation, Germain is somewhat reassured. Maybe it was a peaceful death, after all. In the photos, he notices the body's position when it was found, an arm hooked onto a branch, as if to break a fall. The picture, suggesting the woman's final struggle, wrenches at his heart.

But what upsets him most is Madame Victoria's face. Based on the available data, experts were able to produce a rough portrait. Curly brown hair, high cheekbones, faded features, she seems to stare at him in disappointment, and Germain believes he recognizes her. Was she a patient resigned to never getting well again and whom he'd neglected? Was it his fault she'd gone out to die on the knoll? Had he inadvertently administered the wrong drug? At other times she reminds him of his mother growing old so far away; he doesn't visit her often enough. After months of hoping, like the investigators, that someone would recognize her face, Germain forces himself to banish his gnawing guilt. He has turned Madame Victoria into the repository of all his regrets, all the times he wasn't equal to the task. A heavy burden to unload on a dead woman that didn't know him.

The years go by. Germain changes work units, his daughter enters high school and he does his best to help her across the muddy terrain of puberty. Madame Victoria has gradually faded from the collective memory and joined the army of ghosts occupying the hospital: elderly amnesiacs, drowned schizophrenics, mothers who died in childbirth. Germain alone still thinks of her every day, each time he goes back to his car at the end of a shift, but he is not sad. Now a guardian angel looks out from the little hill, gazes benevolently on the city that gave her a few green sticks of wood to protect her final moments. As for the skeleton lying in a cardboard coffin in the basement of a police station, it would have willingly accepted this box as its final resting place, but for a research team from the University of Ottawa.

More than ten years after Madame Victoria's death, her hair is what interests the researchers this time around. Using new technologies, they manage to extract a slew of fresh information from the robust filaments that have remained intact. Once analyzed, each of the forty-three centimetres of fibre brings to light one month of the anonymous dead woman's last years. What emerges is that Madame Victoria had moved seven times in the space of three years, going southward from the north of the province. In addition, she suffered from a mineral deficiency possibly symptomatic of a serious disease.

The information is shared and distributed throughout the country, but no one is able to identify her. For Germain, all the fuss and repeated failures do nothing but rub salt into the wound. He wishes they would leave Madame Victoria in peace now. After all, she may have wanted to die unobtrusively. Maybe she'd sought anonymity and solitude on purpose. And surely the whole circus over her bones must rankle her spirit longing for just a little silence so it can detach itself from this mountain pierced by such a heavy cross.

Then, as Germain looks out at the canopy of trees and the roofs that speckle Mount Royal, he thinks again. What she wants is for someone to speak her name.

Victoria Outside

OUTDOORS IS A MESS. Chaotic winds shake the air, snow is blowing in every direction, ice and thaw fight it out for control of the ground, clouds swirl overhead, the window is frozen shut. She presses her hand against the pane, waits for the water to spread out between her palm and the glass, and places her eye in front of the gap to look at the mayhem outside. She draws her bathrobe tighter around her ribcage as if to warm the landscape, to find comfort in the feeling of being sheltered from everything. Outside is outside. Inside is a nest, a knot, the earth's axis. A solid heat holds them, her and the little guy. She hears him wriggling. She steps toward him with a smile. On the windowpane, the frost fills in the gap by weaving stars that slowly merge.

She believes she's not asleep anymore. She doesn't think she slept last night or the night before or the one before that. Nor did she sleep during the day, though she has no recollection at all of what she did while the little guy was napping. Yet she's sure she dreamed three days ago – her baby had sharp teeth and webbed fingers – but God knows how long it takes for the brain to produce a dream, maybe just a few seconds.

Earlier, she lay down knowing he always naps for two or three hours after nursing at noon, the time when the will gives up and the scarce February light brushes against the living room wallpaper. She wanted to let herself go, but the child makes such weird sounds in his sleep, squeals and whistles that give the impression he's choking, despite the nurse's assurances that this is normal. These noises seek her out in the place where her tiredness strives to win out; they jostle her body as though numerous little wires were attached to her skin. Now she's nothing but a big puppet that can easily be set trembling, brought to her feet at feeding time, made to sway back and forth to soothe the infant's colic pains.

She would so much like to go out for a breath of air, but the winter won't let her. It has snowed constantly ever since the delivery. At first she was too weak to even think of setting foot outside. When she closed her eyes she could swear an artillery shell had punched a hole through her belly. But that was weeks ago and she still can't bring herself to bundle up the baby, pull on her boots, cut a path through to the poorly cleared street, and then walk over to the convenience store, with its meagre, stale-looking goods. The outside world has nothing to offer her anymore.

All that matters from now on can be found in this tiny apartment that smells of wet diapers and Zincofax. The only adult she's talked to since she got back is the grocery deliveryman, who comes to her door with red splotches on his face, as if the winter has slapped him. She tells him her name is Victoria, since it makes no difference now what her name is. Her mother, her sister—they don't call. Her friends? She never gave them her new address. She chats with her baby as an excuse to talk to herself, for launching into long monologues meant to confirm in her own mind that she made the right choice. She cries every day.

Running away to Quebec City or Montreal held no attraction for her. Unlike so many of her friends, she never hated the place where she grew up. She never said, "Sault-au-Mouton—what a dump!" or yearned for the noisy grid of the big city streets. To her, Montreal, which she'd visited only once, was where people ended up after ditching the idea that the world could be a beautiful place. The one thing that let the city breathe was the mountain. Even the river was dirty, its shores obliterated, as if the waterway were a shameful wrinkle that needed to be concealed. Nothing like what the river becomes on the North Shore. At Sault-au-Mouton the Saint Lawrence is pure prowess, a tour de force. The continent's rippling banner.

She could not imagine living far from all that. Which is why, when it became clear that her decision meant she no longer existed for her family, she crossed over. Going from the North Shore to the Lower Saint Lawrence, only the switched position of sunrise and sunset on the water seems strange. She has no memory of ferrying across; she simply strode over the river in her seven-league boots, weighed down by a seven-month belly and a bagful of old clothes.

She's a good mother, she knows this, though it does come as a bit of a surprise. She'd been told so often that at sixteen she'd be incapable of caring for a child, she ended up believing it. But from a sort of mental lookout produced by her fatigue, she can see herself in action. She is patient. Steady. Not given to discouragement. She sings, she washes, she watches, she feeds. She does what needs to be done, certain that she'll go on doing so, even if her fat melts away, sloughed off with all this milk that spills out of her. She'll become another kind of creature, a bird or possibly a dragonfly, something light that eats almost nothing, that buzzes over the surface of the world and rests even in mid-flight. The universe is shrinking by the minute.

Her baby has grown. He, too, has a name she never uses; she calls him my sweetie, my darling, my treasure.

My heaven, my pot of gold, my little starburst. He smiles, gums his fist, grabs his foot and shakes it bewilderedly, as if the limb did not belong to him. She presses her mouth against his stomach and blows; his colour-shifting eyes open wide. She glides the tip of her finger along the meanders of his minuscule ear, and he turns his head, smiling as if he'd just been told a secret. He sucks, he nibbles, he drools. He babbles and she unlearns how to speak. The delivery man keeps on bringing her groceries; he is less flushed but just as flustered on her doorstep, perhaps because she has stopped using known words. Maybe she's learned the language of elves, their prattle full of small miracles.

She continues to bleed. The nurse says this isn't normal, that she is exhausted and must eat red meat, go out and breathe in the approach of spring and of the fishing that will soon start up again a few blocks from her house. She thinks of Victor, of his arms hauling in the nets and tossing fish as firm as muscles. His hands grasping the heavy ropes, his body directing the boats, the tides, and the miraculous catches. Right now he must be standing on a deck beside his father, repairing cracks and cleaning rusted portholes, breathing in the hope of the coming season, the nearing of the great shoals. She still dreams of lying down with him and drinking every inch of his skin.

He said, "You do as you like, I'll give you what you need. Don't ask anything else of me. Here's some money—do what you want with it. The rest, I've got no time for."

Soon after, she realized he'd chosen another, whose belly hadn't swelled up, that he would never admit to his father he'd gotten the girl from Sault-au-Mouton pregnant, and that it wouldn't be so easy for him to become a man. She left without telling him where she was going. Sure, she still loves him, loves whatever she recognizes of him in her son's face. She never wants to speak to him again.

Her mother had said, "If you become a mother now you'll never be a woman. You'll always be lagging behind, depending on everyone else. Having a child means coming to a stop. You can't stop before you've finished doing what you have to do. What you have to do to be an adult." It's true. She still doesn't have her driver's licence. She can't cook. She hasn't finished school, and she wouldn't be able to fill out a tax return. But contrary to her mother's prediction, she doesn't depend on anyone. That's the condition she set for herself to have this child. Everyone was against it, so she did it alone.

At night, the little one sleeps for a longer time. Three, sometimes four hours in a row. She still wakes up every two hours, like an animal trained to stand guard, heavy-eyed, dense heat throbbing under her skin. She rises, tries to tidy up a little. The objects in her apartment are as light as goose down, so adrift that they settle somewhere else as soon as she's put them back where they belong. In the middle of the night she fixes herself some bread and jam, which she eats standing by the window. She thinks she can hear the crash of the spring breakup as the ice batters the shoreline, the grind of twisted metal deep below the surface, when the shipwrecks grind their teeth. Spring is on its best behaviour but she's knows it's too soon to celebrate. There's always a relapse when everybody is sure it's over.

The only one who hadn't condemned her decision was her father. That's how he was, irresponsible and muddled, brimming with feelings of love that would well up chaotically without always reaching the people who were counting on him. He had many flaws but he could never greet the arrival of a new life with anything but joy. He would have kissed her on the forehead, he would have said "my big girl," adding something about the ton of happiness that was about burst into their lives. He would have uncorked a bottle, insisting she make an exception and share a toast with him, taken her to Forestville and spent his pay on little yellow, blue, and green pyjamas.

Too bad he missed this. If he weren't crammed inside an urn he would have given her a reason to stay. She would have moved in with him, and the others eventually would have come to terms with it. Her mother would have realized how well she cares for her baby. Her friends would have paused their cycle of quarrels and faded love affairs to gush about her newborn's beautiful agate-coloured eyes. Her sister would have agreed, for once, to tear herself away from her beloved campus to spend her vacations in the village and help her remember those wonderful lullabies that melt in your mouth and float above the crib. Victor would have left his new lover on seeing how kind, strong, and brave his son's mother was. She smiles as she imagines her triumph, although she knows things would never have turned out that way.

Love is exponential and she anticipates the moment when her heart will explode. When she harks back to what she felt for her baby just after he was born, it seems to pale in comparison with how complex, how intense her feelings have since become. Whenever she thinks she's reached a plateau, to her astonishment she finds her adoration rising even higher; each time her child accomplishes some new feat her motherly love soars, and on and on it goes. When she hugs him, her cheeks glow red, like a sweetheart. Sometimes it seems she can still feel him kicking inside her. He's both inside and outside. He is everywhere.

The neighbours are getting curious, stopping on her landing as they go downstairs, ears on the alert when they come back up. The creaking of the building sends out messages, questions, suppositions that stay poised on their lips. They're old and grey or young and plump, they whisper in their bathtubs, the murmur crawls along the plumbing, shuts itself inside the kitchen cabinets. Victoria accepts the idea they are talking about her, knows she'll have to come out one day, greet them, introduce her baby to them, let them pinch his cheek. But not right away. She's still bleeding and winter isn't over yet.

In fact, it has started snowing again. There's over a foot of it on the ground as she plunges her hands into the greasy water to wash things that all seem unnecessary to her. The infant is fidgeting in his playpen while he waits for his meal. By the time she sits down to nurse a new layer of snow has covered the pavements that were shovelled just an hour ago. Victoria shrugs as she cuddles her baby against her stomach. It's nice and warm in here. She pats his back, wipes his chin, sings a soothing tune, and kisses him on his eyelids by way of saying good night. Then she nestles into her armchair to watch the storm. The snowflakes fall so thickly, as if someone were shaking the fluff out of a piece of clothes in front of the window. Numbness comes over her, a huge, irresistible fatigue such as she hasn't felt for months. She curls up and goes to sleep.

She sleeps for six hours. Seven hours. Ten hours. The morning finds her aching from a whole night spent in that uncomfortable position. She stretches and watches the daylight creeping in and she doesn't understand. It snowed. She slept. Slept far too long.

The child is still lying on his back, his blanket barely creased. His hands are closed as though hiding precious gems, and his arms are perfectly still. Perfectly still. She lays her hand on his round stomach. Perfectly still.

She knows such things happens sometimes, but you must keep them at a distance, at the far end of a pole, an idea pinned up in a corner of your head that you never visit. You mustn't think of it even if you're always thinking of it. The greater your love, the greater your fear, the more you must be convinced that nothing can harm you.

He doesn't move. His chest doesn't rise. Her finger under his little nose doesn't find the damp warmth she expects. His foot inside the woollen sock is cold. After a very long time, she takes hold of his body, and right then, at that moment, there can be no doubt anymore. Her baby is as light and limp as a doll, like a lifeless treasure.

She lies down on the floor, places him next to her and says, "Come on, my dove, my puppy, you can do it. Say something to mommy, anything. Squeeze mommy's finger. Open your eyes, my love. Look at mommy. See how I much I love you, how much we love each other. We have to stay together always, always." But he stays as light and cold as winter coming back when everyone thought it was over. Her whole body is ripped apart. Everything drains out of her.

She must have screamed because the neighbours came knocking. The scream must have worried them, because they called the fire department. She fights for the longest time to keep them from taking her baby. "We have to examine him, miss." A man holds her in his arms with a painful sort of tenderness to restrain her. A first responder palpates her baby's limbs for a few minutes, and it seems to her that he has revived, but it's an illusion. They let her take back her child, rock him, tell him again all the secrets that mothers weave for their children. The nurse arrives, gives her an injection, then nothing. When Victoria comes to, her little one has vanished, and she is empty.

She sets out on foot. What else can she do? She puts on her seven-league boots and goes out of the house that she hasn't left for three months. The village looks strange to her, different from how it was when she arrived. As though the streets had been twisted, the houses shrunk. Even the sky is disfigured, and she wonders how the geese will manage their crossing, this year.

The ferry isn't running yet, so she keeps on walking. She goes without eating or sleeping, wasting away en route to Trois-Pistoles and La Pocatière, until she sees the sky clearing over Île d'Orléans and Quebec City. She marches across the bridge, continues on toward Sainte-Anne-de-Beaupré without saying a prayer, passes La Malbaie and Tadoussac, until she finally climbs the hill at Sault-au-Mouton.

Her mother doesn't smile when she sees her. She utters her name, arches her eyebrows in disbelief, knits her brow; Victoria says her name is Victoria now. Her mother wants to bathe her, feed her, wrap something warm around her, but Victoria refuses. She says, "I'm fine, the little one is fine, I just wanted to see you, I wanted to tell you how great I'm getting along," then she bursts into sobs. Her mother guides her to a bed redolent of laundry and a roller coaster childhood, and Victoria sleeps for four days. When she awakens, her mother tells her she's learned "of the child's passing," referring in those ceremonious terms to the death of the most important person in her daughter's life. Victoria hurls a glass at her face. He's not dead.

She looks for Victor in the harbour, to no avail. The bad weather keeps the sailors well away from the shore. She goes to his house, to the poolroom, and finds him at last on his ATV at the sand quarry among a dozen boys ready to crack their spines just to hear the roar of their engines and send the flea-ridden sand flying. She watches them for an hour until they start to head home. A cigarette pinched between his lips, boots kicking up gravel with every step, Victor is about to walk past without seeing her. She plants herself in the middle of the road, and the small group looks up at her. Her eyes meet his but Victor remains impassive. He doesn't recognize her. She has wasted away to the point where her features have gotten lost. No one knows her anymore.

Nights on the road are rough; the floodwaters have filled the ditches, the only place she can find shelter and rest. Otherwise she would be visible from the road and vulnerable to harassment. She doesn't want to be harassed. She wants to stretch out on her back and wish the geese safe journey, and pray that the grasses grow tall and fragrant, and for her baby to be brought back to her. Despite the dampness she stays as dry and brittle as a wisp of straw. Her wound is gone, the bleeding has stopped, there is nothing left of her little one. She would so much like to still be in pain, to feel in her bones the huge tear of his birth. All that remains now is her tiredness, a state she carefully maintains, like those who nurture their drunkenness or emaciation. It has stopped raining on the North Shore. The forests are hatching an army of insects to pepper the summer with tiny stingers.

The days are long by the time she reaches Quebec City. She tells herself that all this light will help her find her baby. Intent on building up her strength, Victoria starts to forage behind restaurants and bakeries, feeding on stale bread. She huddles next to walls to eat, focused and methodical, sometimes falling asleep in spite of herself and waking up covered with trash and droppings, as if men and birds had taken her for a discarded bag.

At the university, she begins to search for her sister. The few people she comes across look at her askance. For a few days she camps out on the deserted grounds but fails to find the main gate, the drawbridge. Finally, a gardener provides the key to the puzzle: "summer vacations." The campus has been abandoned, and her sister is probably trekking across the Andes or the Sahel desert, looking for someone to save. Yet there is so much to be done right here, hard by the oldest French-language higher learning establishment in the Americas.

From then on Victoria goes into free fall. She sleeps anywhere she can, preferably on the Plains of Abraham or in a park if no one comes to evict her; otherwise, it's under an overpass or in an alley full of spoiled cats and regal whores. The hookers always give Victoria a friendly greeting and their graciousness cleanses her somewhat. During the day, she combs through the city, certain that her little one can't be very far. She sharpens her sense of hearing, on the alert for the slightest squeal, the piping voice that she would hear even in a hurricane.

When spoken to she talks about nothing else but the lost baby that she has to rescue from the chaos of the world. He must be hungry, she explains, and she needs to find him before he falls into the wrong hands. Some turn their backs on her, others try to reason with her. A very small and precious minority express their sympathy and sometimes offer to help. "If I see a baby with grey-agate eyes I'll let you know right away, I promise." Their words warm her heart; it's good to know there's a small army of allies on the lookout in the great City of Quebec.

With the arrival of winter come new pains, gnawing at her extremities, feet, fingers, ears. Her allies clothe her, reassure her: her baby is snug as a bug, not to worry, he's warm and waiting for her in a comfortable little bed somewhere, protected from the blowing snow. Victoria nods, thrusts her hands into the fetid old mittens that keep her alive. Sometimes she's brought to shelters, crowded dormitories where she's instructed to eat at mealtime, wash at shower time, sleep at bedtime, and keep out of the icy winds that, they tell her, cast people like her out of the world of the living. She runs away as soon as she can, unable to remain cut off from the open spaces full of the sounds and threads that connect mothers and children. She goes to hang around church squares and the aromatic entrances of cafés. She's no longer afraid or sad.

The searching takes her from winter to spring, from summer to autumn, to another spring, another winter; she lets the wheel spin without keeping count. Her hair turns brittle, her fingernails split, her lips become raw, and her skin sags, but she is still just as young. Her body crumbles but stays whole, becomes gnarled but stays smooth. Sometimes she senses Victor watching her from afar, and she strikes a pose to show him her bum, her smiling breasts, her lively mouth like a fish that's just been thrown back into the water. She is thin. It was inevitable—she's become an arrow and her whole being points north.

It happens in the frozen depths of winter. Her pure and weary body brings her the answer the city could not give her. She is huddled under a warm air vent outside a bar sending out all the joys of the world. This is when she feels the first tingle. In her belly, in the uterus she had kept empty and prepared for everything. A bubble bursts, a butterfly wing grazes the surface of the universe. She places her purplish hands on her abdomen and raises her eyes toward the dazzling precision of the stars. "Stay calm, Victoria. Wait till you're sure."

When spring arrives there's no room for doubt. Her belly has swelled with an unmistakable little bump whose movements can't be ignored any longer. Already the salutary pains tug at her and the breath that rises from the life stirring there confirms what she should have guessed: she should have searched for her little one not in the streets of a city trodden by her own history but right inside her, where he had taken shelter and waited for the right moment to signal his presence, to let his mother know he had never left.

Buoyed by this good news, Victoria sets out again. She heads north, where the cold is direct and the light is slant. She carries her baby to the places of his earliest days, knowing she is strong enough this time to take him around, to show him the pliant landscape, the fields and strands that belong to him, to walk with him for years.

He is born at night in a stand of firs as tight as a tunnel, and she holds him closely without seeing him. He isn't sticky like the first time, or as noisy or hungry, and she felt no pain. As soon as he's out, he breaks free of her grasp like a young partridge eager to take wing. He twirls around her while she catches her breath. She curls up and touches her belly, which she notices is still hard and full. She's at once empty and full. The baby nuzzles up against her, and his caresses come from within her and from out there all at the same time. He's both inside and outside.

They live facing the wind, and each day they celebrate their reunion. They lie down on the oblong beaches, cover themselves with dead leaves, and Victoria regains the kind of sleep she likes: blunt and overpowering. In the morning, the little one snuggles inside her hood and they set out in search of food. She chews grass and serves it to him on her thumbnail. A hundred times a day she strokes her son's cheeks and kisses his innumerable fingers. He's in the water she drinks and in the leather of her soles. He is everywhere.

They have just crossed the river when she's arrested. The officers explain that she can't sleep outside, this isn't Montreal, and there are laws, and places for people like her. They take her, along with her baby, to one such place. The bed stinks, the window is tiny, and the water in the toilets is foul and won't swirl when you flush. Fortunately, the little guy has no trouble slipping under the doors and goes out to play in the fresh air whenever he likes. Victoria continues to caress him in her belly, where the salutary tugs persist. She refuses to eat and doesn't answer the questions that are put to her.

Grumpy women come to examine every inch of her. They squeeze, grope, ask her to cough, to spread her legs, they take her blood and her urine, and one of them even dares to press down on her belly as though, under the shirt and skin, she had seen a little angel capering about in his mother's pink waters. She is shut in for weeks. The little one grows impatient and Victoria, weaker. To thrive, they need the vastness of the countryside and the cool of the night. A thousand times she thinks of escaping. Her fatigue bars the way.

On the morning when two square-shouldered, clean-shaven men come for her, her wound suddenly reopens. She screams and protests. The little one hasn't come back yet. "We have no choice, Madame. Montreal is the place for you. Your cancer is too complicated for the local hospital." She has no idea what they're talking about and wraps her hands over her belly as they drag her to an enormous vehicle. She cries the whole way, a seven-hour drive; she doesn't want to go to Montreal, they're driving too fast, the little guy will never be able to catch up. As they pass hideous, reeking factories, she sobs even louder. Her only consolation is to feel him lodged in her belly. Over and over she says, "Never apart again. Never apart again."

They take her to a building perched on a mountain. It looks like an ancient castle surrounded by woods and she finds some comfort in this. She waits in a room overlooking the woods, until a lady finally comes to speak to her. She says she is Dr. Eon, that Victoria is under her care, that it's complicated because she has no papers but they'll make do without because her life is at risk. She announces they will open her belly to remove a lump of tissue that is trying to kill her. Victoria is frightened, she hesitates; can she share her secret with this woman? The doctor has eyes of different colours, and this reassures her. She explains that she's willing to have the operation, but they must be very careful with the baby in her belly because she loves him so much and doesn't want to lose him.

"It's not a baby, Madame. It's a tumour. It's quite possible you feel a tingle that may seem like something moving, but it's absolutely impossible that you're pregnant. Given your age." So Victoria starts to scream, refuses to let them cut her open, flings anything within reach at Dr. Eon. More women arrive, grab her wrists and ankles, strap her down, Victoria howls, calls them murderers. They give her an injection.

She wakes up feeling that forty years have just elapsed. The restraints are gone and her abdomen is bound up with a straggly bandage. She is not in pain. But the moment she touches her stomach, she understands. They've taken her baby from her. She can't even manage to cry, and from her parched tongue she knows for sure they've drugged her. Outside, the light is long, full as a bottle on the sea; the summer chants a cheeky nursery rhyme. She tries to get dressed, to slip a foot out of the bed but the bandage pins her down. She's been sliced, paralyzed. She pisses on the sheet.

The nurse who washes her and changes her dressings tries to find out if someone will be waiting for her when she's discharged. "My son." She asks where Victoria plans to go. "Out." The nurse doesn't contradict her and brings back leaflets about shelters that look like all the places where Victoria had stayed in Quebec City. She guesses that, once again, they have no intention of letting her choose. As soon as she's back on her feet they'll force her to go to some other place where her son won't be able to find her. She can't let that happen.

At night she gets up noiselessly to exercise. She has done enough walking in her lifetime to understand which muscles must stay strong, which nerves must be kept limber. She trains. She wants to get back into shape. Because the only thing she knows for sure is that if he's not inside anymore, he's outside. During the day she makes a show of being weak and in pain, and asks to be given tranquilizers, which she then spits into her pillowcase along with the other drugs she's been ordered to swallow. She pretends to be drowsy, shaky, miserable, and no one is onto her.

A lid of clouds sits over the ground as if to keep the night quiet. She decides this is the right moment. Her legs are firm, her belly is entirely free of pain; her belly may be dead but she is very much alive. She slips out of her nightgown and into a uniform pilfered the previous night. In the faded mirror, she looks at herself for the first time in ages. She's a wreck, yet ecstatic to know her treasure is waiting for her somewhere. Her head spins and her heart races.

Wearing slippers, she treads silently down the corridor. She finds her way, the door opens and presents her with the outside as others surrender whole countries. It all belongs to her. After a few hesitant steps on the asphalt she hurries toward the trees. They're thin and scattered, but they'll do. If she can get across Montreal going from tree to tree without ever touching concrete, she'll be saved. But she's prepared to crawl under the pavement, in the sewers full of rats as bloated as billionaires, to be reunited with her son.

The slope is steep and the breeze is warm. Victoria is reminded she has long hair when she feels it brushing her back, and she smiles. Never has she felt this free. She climbs to the top of the knoll. From this vantage point she can see Montreal's complicated roofs, its cracked avenues, its resolute inhabitants, and she tells herself she may have been wrong about this place. The city hums with tenderness. The branches around her start to dance and something commands her to stay put. This exactly where she ought to be.

His laughter is what she hears first. Laughter so exultant that it bursts out like a cough, fitful and uncontrollable. The laughter of a baby discovering for the first time the organ that gives voice to joy. Victoria lifts her head. She can see nothing now, as a million colours explode before her eyes. His smell reaches her, as tender as butter and sugar surrendering to each other, a blend of eiderdown and saliva, and she succumbs to the giddiness brought on by this extraordinary scent. At last, he arrives and leaps into her arms with such force that she topples over backward. She hugs him and murmurs, "You've come back, you've come back" with endless admiration for this brave boy who was able to find her on an island of labyrinths.

In the dead leaves, she holds the small, bare head tightly near her heart; two round feet climb up on her hip; he nuzzles up against his mother. Victoria feels light and large, larger and larger. She grows bigger and taller and expands like warm air, like the aroma of good bread. Her son is a little ball nestled against her breast, as Victoria swells and towers over the knoll, the hospital, the mountain, as she spreads through the sky and the streets, through the houses, and to the stars. She is inside, she is outside. She is everywhere.

Victoria Drinks

EVERYTHING STARTS at the throat. The thirst, the cough, the voice. The words that move mountains, the breaths like punches, the burning that comes with every swallow. All the rest proceeds from that pain: the woody aromas, the texture at once subtle and firm, the dry savours that swim to the core of your being. A tiny wound that forges your thoughts, filters colours, sharpens sounds, brings the world into focus.

What does it say about a woman that she drinks Scotch? In a man this would be a sign of determination, strength, refinement. Success. In a woman, the same, plus one more attribute: ambition. Victoria raised her first glass as one might utter a password to gain entry into the holy of holies, where alliances are formed and power is confirmed. The place where ascension becomes possible, amid mahogany and pipe tobacco, thirty metres above the multitudes.

In her teenage years it would have been hard to picture her at such lofty heights. She was not born into one of those families where a learned father eager to pass on his knowledge imparted to his sole descendant the rudiments of Aristotelian philosophy and an uncommon ability to decipher anagrams. In Victoria's house, you learned to darn socks, peel potatoes without lifting the knife, and not answer back to adults. Victoria did not answer to anyone.

In boarding school she kept her distance from the chattering cliques, unable to fathom their frivolity, their puerile humour, their obedience. She hunched over books from which she emerged unappeased and impatient. The sisters' prayers, psalms, and theoretical simplifications failed to satisfy the famished mouth lodged somewhere between her mind and her heart. The days and months streamed past with a slow precision that made Victoria feel as though she were living at the centre of a gigantic clock.

Early in her final year, when the most brainless of her classmates were beginning to dream about the men to whom they would surrender their youth, and the most sensible were preparing for the cloister, Victoria decided to ask the principal for a letter of recommendation in support of her college application.

"What are you going to do there? What about farming?"

The nun eyed her suspiciously. Victoria imagined a future of plowing, mud, swollen udders, and the stench of liquid manure.

"No, Sister."

"And what about marriage?"

Victoria shrugged. Throughout her life she had seen exhausted women married to men for whom it was not enough to burden their wives with yearly pregnancies; they themselves were a burden the women had to shoulder while remaining under their sway. Women who were captives of a decision taken in haste thirty years earlier because it was spring, the birds were singing, and the pollen had driven them temporarily mad.

"I . . . I'm not very domestic-minded. I'd like to go on with my studies. To go further."

Her reply drew a rare grin from the all-powerful mother superior.

"Well, I've waited a long time to discover one who's interested in learning."

The next day Victoria found herself in possession of a flattering tissue of lies that praised her faith, modesty, and remarkable intellectual achievements, thereby liberating her from the misery of the countryside and the benighted suitors her parents had lined up for her. She was seized by a vague but stubborn intuition: she must take full advantage of this unhoped-for opportunity. Clutching the letter in her fingers, she uttered the first and only oath she would ever take: she would become something different. Something that did not yet exist, and which would surpass all else.

She moved to the metropolis, a city seething with a wild yet friendly energy from which Victoria, however, was almost entirely cut off by the austere walls of the teachers' college for young women. This establishment trained its students to become schoolteachers, governesses, or spouses who played minuets for their in-laws. But what the college turned out to be mainly was a hotbed of quarrels. For Victoria's fellow students were not primarily concerned with reading ancient texts but with securing a best friend. So, turning her back on the dramatic intrigues that grew out of that necessity, Victoria concentrated unenthusiastically but rigorously on her studies.

Every other Sunday the young women were allowed to venture out into the volatile winds of Montreal. For Victoria, those days were a blessing. Detaching herself from the other students, she went out to explore the ordinary neighbourhoods, to immerse herself in the sultry intimacy of their inhabitants. It was not the people themselves that interested her so much as the effervescence of their closeness, the untidy world that they constituted. Among the outcrops of English and the yellow lustre of Montreal French, she made her greatest discovery: newspapers. Their smeary pages made her feel she was at last moored to the world, not as before through the theory and pious gaze of the clergy but by facts, the simple, lucid enunciation of the truths teeming around her. At night she devoured the newspapers under her blankets, deaf to the murmurs of her dormitory mates. She had found her home.

A week after she graduated, Victoria, wearing short hair, pants, and a sober blouse, sat down at her typewriter for the first time. Hired by a major newspaper as a stenographer, she lost no time in overstepping the bounds of her position. Amid the jibes of the other secretaries, "Full Stop Victoria" a.k.a. "Mrs. Trousers" furiously underscored spelling mistakes and accosted reporters with a raft of suggestions on how to improve their texts. The journalists quickly forgot their wounded pride and welcomed, even solicited, the advice of this woman, who rescued their articles day after day.

Despite this, she was shut out. As though an invisible barrier stood between the typists tapping away and the ink-and-tobacco redolence of the newsroom. To get closer to the messy, reprobate, garrulous men that she aimed to surpass, Victoria decided to force the door of their sanctuary: the tavern.

A snowstorm was raging. Dressed in a felt coat and a battered hat, she confidently crossed the threshold of l'Ours qui tousse, The Coughing Bear. Immediately, the dampness produced by melted snow and evaporated malt shrouded her as if to soften the gazes suddenly directed at her by a hundred men. Unperturbed, she cleaved the dense row of stools and took a seat. The room fell silent. Only her neighbour to the right, already well in his cups, muttered unhappily from time to time. No one at l'Ours qui tousse had ever seen a woman stay for more than thirty seconds, just long enough to retrieve her husband. That one of her sex should actually sit down at the bar was so absurd her bewildered colleagues chose to ignore her.

The evening might have continued like this down to the dregs, with the men politely sipping their pints of Dow and the barman content to offer Victoria a spruce beer, when the solution appeared in the form of a mug overflowing with ale. Nicknamed The Trouble, the huge mug was impossible to get completely clean and was reserved for the unlucky, the cuckolds, the losers, anybody who one way or another was being shown the door. In the absence of someone less fortunate, The Trouble was allotted that day to Victoria's neighbour, a reporter who had been chastised by his editor-in-chief for a factual mistake.

When the fellow tried to grasp the mug and his hand came down wide of the mark, Victoria had a sudden stroke of inspiration.

"He's had enough to drink. I'll help him out," she declared.

With her customary resolve, she seized The Trouble, raised it to her lips, and proceeded to quaff the pint and a half of beer contained in the unwholesome jar. Her experience with this drink was limited to the drops her father would leave at the bottom of his glass, of which she had retained a sour and dismal memory. She first had to overcome that feeling and then deal with the froth that flooded her mouth, the sensation of being instantly replete, to discern at last the rare subtleties of the local brew, the sugars and bitterness that lend it a slight degree of dignity. As the crowd looked on dumbfounded, Victoria downed the whole thing in one go, regally set The Trouble down again, let out a brief belch, and announced, "Drinks for everyone. This round's on me."

From that day forward, deaf to the stenographers' snide remarks, Victoria sat down each night at a table in the pub, where, realizing her natural resistance to alcohol, she drank while keeping intoxication at bay and let the fact she was woman gradually be forgotten. A few weeks on, as if by magic, her supervisors took notice of the woman who was rescuing everyone's articles and discreetly suggesting stories to the assignment editor, a number of which had ended up on the front page. It was a small step from rewriting the reports she had proposed to producing her own pieces, a step the paper's management took with the heady impression of crossing the Strait of Magellan. Victoria was the first female reporter in the history of the daily.

She began to work at a frantic pace, arriving at dawn and leaving long after the paper had gone to press. On the pretext of lending a hand she did a little of everything and gained experience in every job, especially the top-level positions. The years went by, but the hollow space at the core of her being that she strived to fill with achievements both great and small was still not full.

One night the publisher summoned Victoria to his office, apparently surprised at his own initiative. The news editor, a tired man whose obesity aggravated his asthma and vice versa, was retiring. For a long time now, when Victoria had finished her articles she would unobtrusively come over to assist him and step in whenever discouragement and bourbon got the best of the old man. She flitted around the plates, made child's play of the most crowded layouts, and raised her glass with him once the edition was finally wrapped up.

Sounding like someone christening a ship, the publisher offered her the position.

"You're young, but you know this job better than anyone. We said to ourselves, let's give our little Victoria a chance."

Victoria took the proffered cup, which contained a shimmering splash of amber liquid.

"I work harder than all my colleagues put together. Chance has nothing to do with it, sir."

She clinked her glass against that of her stunned superior and poured a thread of alcohol between her lips. Her first taste of Scotch. The liquor inundated her mouth like a conquering army.

She had never felt love or desire or anything intense except her calculated ambitions, from which she derived precious little sensual pleasure. That first mouthful of single malt was her first encounter with true passion, with the fervour that carries away whole nations and divides continents. She drained her glass as the bemused publisher looked on, her body alert, her mind more razor-sharp than ever. She was an arrow resolutely pointed north.

Nothing could hold her back. After running the news desk for a few years she moved to the assignment desk before finally joining the management. At every new level she smashed a wall that she was the first woman to break through. She did not look back, gave no more thought to the stenographers, who from now on kept their sneers to themselves, nor did she pay any attention, whenever she passed by there, to the college that had given her nothing but the urge to escape from the world it proposed. She raised high her glass of whisky, closed her eyes, and sucked in the fruits of her obstinacy.

She was given a secretary. Had Olivia been an uneducated, overly made-up woman she would have been easy to hate. But she looked nothing like the cliché that Victoria had always despised. Tall, bright, and boyish, Olivia spent her breaks reading progressive journals or writing suffragist leaflets. She admired Victoria no end and took advantage of every opportunity to ask about her work, her youth, her ideals, unable to accept that her boss's actions were not underpinned by any grand principle.

"Do you realize you've paved the way for the women of Quebec?"

"No. I paved my own way, and sometimes I'm sorry I didn't lob a grenade behind me."

"But my whole generation is in your debt. You're a pioneer."

"Exactly. And pioneers don't travel across continents to wait for the others to catch up. They do it to find some peace and get away from social clubs."

But Olivia was right. Over the years more and more women had made their way into the newsroom. The young female journalists were looking for a mentor and they all turned to Victoria. But she was used to managing a male staff and found herself at a loss for how to deal with their apprehensions, their hesitations, and their muffled sobs in the washroom. Her bafflement soon changed into annoyance and then hostility. Seeing the editor's lack of sympathy toward the newcomers, Olivia took it upon herself to welcome them. On the strength of her boss's authority, she provided advice and guidance on the world of the newspaper, gradually transforming the waiting room of her office into a gynaecium abuzz with complaints about anything and everything. An exasperated Victoria finally exploded:

"If you can't come to work without whining you're not cut out to be journalists. Murders, plots, disasters—in a word, reality—is not for the faint-hearted. Next time I hear anyone so much as squeak, I'm throwing her out."

While the terrified young women scuttled out of the office, Olivia glared at her supervisor.

"You could try to be more considerate. After all, they're the ones who will be taking over from you."

"I certainly hope not!" Victoria exclaimed.

Her assistant let out an irate sigh.

"Is there anything else?" Victoria barked.

Olivia frowned. "You shouldn't drink so much."

"Excuse me?"

"Liquor makes you cruel."

"It's not 'liquor.' It's Scotch. And if it didn't exist your little friends would already have been fired, and you too. Starting now, your job here is to answer the telephone, organize my schedule, and keep that brood of hens away from me."

Victoria felt satisfied as she sank into her armchair. Yet what she had just said was not quite true. The Scotch did not help her tolerate others, and she did not drink out of despair or dependence. She drank out of love. Her goal was neither to forget nor to feel numb or satiated. She simply wished to make contact with that elusive, shifting, multiform essence that understood her, just as she herself intuited Scotch. But it was out of the question for her to explain this to anyone, especially not her secretary.

From that day on Olivia adopted a steadfast coldness that suited Victoria in every respect. Bolstered by the support of her secretary, she took the daily in new directions, crushed her adversaries, and became an integral part of the complex networks shaping the province's destiny. From behind the shaded windows of her office she orchestrated the downfall of a politician, the ascension of a starlet, and the disclosure of a scandal. She dominated her world with neither pity nor cruelty but with blade-like precision.

The more power she acquired the more she avoided the limelight, shunning the galas for the tranquility of her office and decisions made quietly, when everyone else was asleep. Before going on to the next matter at hand, she would pour herself a few shots of Islay or Highland or Speyside, indulging her pleasure without compunction, getting drunk as if by accident, as a side effect of the kiss bestowed on her by her high-priced bottles. But she left her most precious Scotch untouched. The flask of Eon Special Reserve remained at all times in the inside pocket of her jacket, close to her heart. Whenever her colleagues teased her about it, her face took on a stony expression.

"Come on, Vic, how about sharing a little? We've just bought our top competitor!"

"It's a one-of-a-kind blend, and it's mine alone."

"But never tasting a drop of a whisky like that—what a waste!"

"I'll drink it in due course."

She saw wars and trends and inventions come and go, things that were supposed to change the world but left human nature intact. She crossed oceans, stayed in penthouses, ate caviar off the backs of naked women when the boredom of the wealthy had reached that point. She played golf, billiards, and hockey, hunted and killed a bear with her left eye shut and her right eye flashing. She shook hands, was hugged, delivered memorable slaps on the backs of her associates, and, once, a punch to a big oaf in a bowtie who had tried to kiss her. She slept alone and stored her secrets inside her flask of Eon Special Reserve.

Her foes awaited her demise like scientists observing the erosion of a cliff. But they were unaware that Victoria, now over seventy, had already begun to erode, yet her heart, clean as a knife in cold water, and her alcohol-soaked nerves, let nothing show through. Only Olivia suspected the lesions and vapours that festered inside her boss, but she kept mum and got rid of the bloodstained tissues that Victoria carelessly dropped into the wastepaper basket.

One morning in May, her body suddenly failed. After a long night of work, Victoria stood up and, immediately, the room went soft; the hard facts of the floor, the walls, the objects that she had always taken for granted, slipped away. As she collapsed she tried to grab something to break her fall, but for the first time reality proved inadequate. Finding nothing more solid than herself, she clasped her own elbows and fainted.

On waking, she found herself in a drab room, parched and horizontal, tubes sprouting from every imaginable orifice. The bed on which she was stretched out smelled of the nameless multitude that had lain there before her. The corridor buzzed with activity that was at once hectic and sluggish, as if the surfeit of tasks was not enough to erase the weariness of the people performing them.

Over the more than seven decades of her lifetime, Victoria had consistently managed to avoid setting foot in a hospital. She had been seen, just once, in a private clinic, but only because she needed sutures and her teammates in the Chamber of Commerce league had refused to stitch her up directly at the hockey rink. As for those institutions crammed with the miseries of humankind in all its density and complexity, she had always given them a wide berth. So how did she end up there, when just a moment ago she had been torpedoing a parliamentary bill concerning the newspaper industry?

A note on her bedside table provided the answer.

I found you lying on the floor this morning. You had fallen and hit your head on the desk. It seems you will have to stay in the hospital for a good while. Don't fret about the paper. I'll take care of everything. Olivia.

"The little bitch," Victoria spat as she crumpled the piece of paper.

"You shouldn't say that!" replied a voice that made her jump.

At the far end of the room an attendant was folding sheets and looking at her in dismay.

"The woman who left that note saved your life. If she hadn't given you first aid you wouldn't be here."

"And you think that's doing someone a favour?"

"It's better than ending up in the morgue," the woman shot back on her way out.

Annoyed, Victoria yanked at the tubes that had been used, it seemed, to tie her down. Her efforts apparently set off an alarm, as three nurses swooped in to restrain her, repeatedly urging her to "calm down, my dear." Continuing to struggle, Victoria thought of Olivia and hated her with a passion. She spent the night sweating and shivering while she pictured the swarm of pretenders jostling each other in front of her office. Toward four in the morning, when her sweat stopped smelling of malt, she grasped the full horror of her captivity. During those first days at the Royal Victoria she tried to escape seven times without ever managing to reach the door of her room. The basic mechanisms of her body seemed to have thrown in the towel. Young doctors talked to her about her liver, her intestines, her esophagus as though they were minefields; they affirmed the absolute necessity of eliminating alcohol from her diet, oblivious to the fact that without alcohol there would be no diet, strictly speaking. She was forced to swallow disgusting meals, which she vomited up on her plate. The housekeepers were the only ones to leave her alone; they went about cleaning her room with a degree of enthusiasm in line with their meagre wages. They were the weak links in the hospital chain and they soon became Victoria's main allies.

In exchange for some paltry bribes they supplied her with bottles that made her days bearable. Deformed by dropsy, her skin yellowed by jaundice, Victoria would steal over to the washroom whenever possible and drink without restraint. Now that the long hours of work that had acted as a rampart between her and the Scotch were gone, what stretched before her was the slope of an unobstructed horizon, a barrier finally knocked down. Her sordid surroundings in no way diminished her delight. Like a tribute to the beauty of the world, the alcohol cancelled out the incontinence, the incivilities, the gastroenterologists, the gowns that exposed her backside. The boredom of being away from the newspaper.

But it could not blot out Olivia's silhouette when she arrived in Victoria's room one dreary morning holding a small package tied up with ribbons. After briefly scanning the room, she went out only to return a moment later.

"Pardon me, I'm looking for Victoria . . ."

"Here I am," the patient cut in.

Olivia, struck dumb, peered at her former boss.

"It's you? Sorry, I . . ."

"Yes, resting has worked wonders."

The secretary approached the bed.

"No improvement?"

"As sharp-eyed as ever."

"Well, at least your morale is holding up."

"Why have you come? To give me absolution? One last embrace after sending me here to rot?"

"Why are you always so mean?"

"Mean? That's what you think of me?" Victoria grinned. "I'm not mean. I simply have no time to lose. People don't interest me."

"Women don't interest you."

"Women have never been of any use to me."

"So what does interest you?"

Victoria took another shot from the bottle stuffed inside a rumpled drawsheet.

"The ascent," she declared casually.

Olivia nodded for a while. Then she slowly took hold of the Aberlour, gently pulled it out of her boss's grip, and raised it to her lips. One quick, emphatic gulp. She replaced the bottle between the patient's swollen fingers.

"I've come to tell you that Gendron has taken over your position again. The whole team thanks you for your work over the years."

She tossed the package on the foot of the bed and left. Victoria knocked back a mouthful of Scotch. Someone else, doing her job. Someone else. Her job. Turning her eyes to the present left behind by Olivia, she reached out and tried to sit up to grasp the thing, which seemed to mock her. It was no use. She finally called out to an attendant who was walking past her room.

The woman sullenly handed the package to Victoria, who somehow succeeded in ripping it open. On a golden plaque were her name, two dates, and a Latin phrase summarizing her entire career. She clenched her jaws so hard it made her ears hum. So the world truly was the voracious, mutable animal that she had always imagined it to be. As soon as a crack appeared the organism spontaneously rearranged itself to fill the empty space and erase all signs of a gap. Someone else had taken over her job.

She drained the bottle of single malt in a few minutes. The great intoxication came down on her habitual gloom like a bludgeon. She managed—as if her body had been waiting for this—to climb down from her bed. Determined though unsteady, she went to the closet and fished out the jacket she had worn on arriving at the hospital. Then she filched a walker, which enabled her to wend her way down the corridors haunted by women in white. They seemed on the verge of grabbing her, of holding her against her will, of turning her into one more docile, defeated, indistinguishable patient. She swore at them. The flask glowed against her breast.

She made her way to the exit without getting lost, as if she had memorized the maze of the hospital's geography. Waiting for her at the other end of the parking lot was a wood. The hill she had chosen overlooked the buildings where a small menagerie bustled in the midst of disease, where human beings stooped over the unwell, where newborns wriggled in the arms of their parents, where family members held each other close and their tears intermingled. She hurried. The holes, the abscesses, the varicose veins, and the lesions were flaring up inside her.

At the foot of the knoll she cast aside her walker. The slope was steep and climbing it took an inordinate amount of time, but Victoria made it to the top as if out of habit. Breathless, she leaned her back against a young birch. The city was spread out at her feet: the roofs and facades that enclosed her former office, the rooms where she had slept opaquely through many nights, the college and, beyond the river, the muddy lands that had witnessed her birth—a landscape she could no longer fathom. For the place where logic and ambition had been in command was now occupied by a dizzy sense of fullness. Placing her hand on her chest, Victoria coughed and felt a hundred vesicles burst in the depths of her throat.

She groped inside her jacket for the flask that had followed her everywhere for the past twenty years. When she lifted the container to her ear and shook it she heard the chime of molten gold. It seemed like rain was splashing down around her, yet she remained dry. An uncommon tenderness washed over her heart and the back of her head. Her vision grew blurry.

Below, the city still throbbed, but Victoria no longer saw it. Her world sat in the palm of her hand. She had retained her primordial thirst, and now it was almost quenched—a feeling of having at once lost and conquered and, especially, of being precisely where she ought to be. Her fingers uncorked the flask. The redolence rose from her Eon Special Reserve like claws lashing out, and the too-sudden joy made her knees buckle. She filled her chest with a final breath of air and turned her face to the sky; ready now for the last triumph, she locked her lips around the mouth of the bottle. She thought she heard a gong ring out somewhere. She drank.

Victoria on Borrowed Time

I BELIEVE WE DIDN'T quite know why we wanted to die. At that age, more than at any other time of life, you want to love, kill, come, suffer, but you don't know why. You react to one desire by responding to another; you try to quench your thirst by lighting a fire, to heal a wound by thrusting your finger into it. I believe we wanted to die of love, which was very silly and at the same time surprisingly clear-sighted for adolescents. How were we to know that if we'd let our passion run its course it would have dissolved after a few years and given way to the humdrum disappointment that unites old couples? We had no idea what lay ahead, yet we wanted to avoid it. Our sadness had sharpened us like arrowheads and we were pointed north. Toward the mine.

He died and I lived, whereas the opposite should have happened. For a long time I thought I was the one who had corrupted him. With no childhood to speak of and no family except those assigned to me by the government, I had never learned to hope. But I had the trills and the alders of the grove, and the purl of the river. I suppose that's what enabled me to bide my time until I met him. He came from another place, from a house as yellow as a Sunday morning egg yolk, as warm as the smell of roasted chicken.

It started in history class, the worst course of all. We were told about the Inquisition, the witches burned at the stake, the African slave trade, the massacre of the American indigenous peoples, the Holocaust. All those horrors coated with a neutral varnish by the Department of Education. Sitting at the desk next to mine, Daniel began to cry while the teacher blithely recounted the death of the last Inca emperor. He wept so softly that it was the tiny plash of his tears on his textbook that caught my attention. The next day I sat down beside him on the bus. He was thin and handsome, he had eyes of different colours, and his hair was dyed the dark shade worn by all unhappy boys. I took his hand in mine and held on to it after that.

We touched each other with the dread and awe once reserved for dragons and horses. He knelt before my bereavements and nightmares and transformed them into small pyres that refused to burn. I kissed every joint, every knot of his frail body, every blow received at random in schoolyards and vacant lots. He fashioned miniature clay figurines meant to reshape my life story and make me into a heroine, and in a hushed voice composed little melodies that I would learn by heart. I've never met anyone else with that kind of imagination and the knack for pouring it into such small forms.

His parents liked me. They would probably have liked anyone interested in spending so much time with their son. I also believe that they pitied me to some extent. And, above all, that they were decent people. I was at their house all the time. After school, for homework. Before supper, to watch the stupid TV shows. Spaghetti on Monday, hamburgers on Friday. Weekend chores that wore us out, with Mr. Borduas cheering us on and laughing at our contorted faces; Christmas holidays with Mrs. Borduas insisting we sing carols in front of the tree. The citrus smell of their car at 10:30 p.m., when they drove me back to the hard-angled house that I was never able to consider my home.

When we turned sixteen, the Borduas decided it was acceptable for me to sleep over, in the same room as their son. If this permission had never been given, things might have gone in a different direction. Our adolescent angst eventually would have subsided. But as is often the case for the sick and the reckless, the night changed everything. Now we could talk for hours on end about the reasons why we thought the human race was doomed, a horrible accident in the history of the world. Under the heavy quilt of his bed, we learned to articulate, dissect, and magnify our despair so that it grew into a creature more solid than ourselves.

We began our last year in high school constantly sleep-deprived, which made us as brittle as dry bread. It was time to make decisions, choose a career, plan our lives—the sort of process that seemed to unfold in a foreign language, according to an indecipherable code. We refused to fill out the forms, to take the tests that were supposed to guide us toward the fields that suited us best, and soon our boycott extended to schoolwork in general. We had no wish to do anything anymore except to be together in his bed, welded into an unintelligible ball, rejecting whatever was not our love.

What happened next should come as no surprise to anyone. That sort of pact was already unexceptional at the time. To realize now how ordinary our situation really was is almost worse than having nurtured such suffering, than surviving the death of the person I loved. To realize that the feelings we thought we were the first to discover were in fact shared by thousands of other teenagers who were too fond of Kurt Cobain or Émile Nelligan or knives.

Some cities have a bridge or a railroad where the trains shoot past. In our town there was the mine. An open pit so massive it took your breath away, long abandoned by the company that had dug it and guarded by derelict fences full of gaps made by curious locals, explorers, or just plain fools looking for a place to get high. As for us, we hung out there to get better acquainted with the void. We would sit down at the edge of the precipice with our stomachs in knots, and our dizziness would get mixed up with the pounding of our hearts. It was the ideal spot to kill yourself.

Unaffected by clichés about November, we chose that month the way budding poets choose to write about the sky and the flowers. We dressed in black. We spent a peaceful night breathing side by side, feeling our pulses, listening to the sound of the life between our two bodies extended like javelins before the final throw. That morning we refused to eat breakfast and Daniel hugged his parents before leaving. He didn't leave them a note. We slipped through the rusted fence and walked to the edge of the pit. There was a lowering sky, the wind was lurking somewhere, the air was still, it was Wednesday and our absence from school must already have been noted. My stomach ached.

Thirty metres below there were rocks piled up like extracted teeth. We held each other's hands very tightly, my left in his right, and I recall being amazed at not feeling any sweat on our skins. He spoke in a solemn voice: "I'm crazy about you. You're the only person I've ever loved, and that will stay true forever." Finding it hard to breathe, I mumbled something similar. Daniel counted to three. The countdown unfolded the way fateful moments always do, stretching out to let our thoughts run free. I heard one-two-three and I felt like laughing—to use that inane signal for such a serious act. I thought, one-two-three, jump in the water, I remembered my first attempts in the pool where I learned to swim, the turquoise world that greeted me, the way it stopped the voices, the song of the robins, and the threats, the strange angles at which the sun entered the water. I saw myself, so small and nervous, frolicking under the surface, untouchable and drifting, one-two-three you're the queen, one-two-three you're a mermaid, one-two-three this instant, the last of your existence, is no different from the ones before. It's a moment just like all the others, no more necessary and no less, no truer and no less. One, two, three. You don't die.

I watched him take an incredible leap above the abyss. I don't think I had ever seen him put as much energy into a single action. He seemed to hover weightlessly and for a split second I believed he would take flight, that he'd won, that he'd made an all-or-nothing bet and was now reaping the gift that human beings had coveted since Icarus. Then he fell. There was a thud so soft it astonished me. No crunching bones, no spewing blood. Just a kind of "poof," like a pile of clothes landing at the foot of the bed. I stood stock-still for a minute. I guess my head was trying to take in what had just occurred. Finally, I shouted his name. He didn't answer. I told myself, "Come on. It's time. Go ahead. Now. You big wimp." Then I thought he might still be alive. I stepped toward the edge. Then an enormous weight came down on me.

"Don't move. Don't move. You're not going anywhere." The man pinned me under his full weight, repeating those words as if to make sure I wouldn't escape. I broke into tears. I cried until the ambulance arrived. The man got up, but I continued to feel his weight on me. The paramedics wrapped me in an aluminum blanket as though I was in danger of hypothermia. They went down to the bottom of the mine and the one who came to announce Daniel's death said, "He's really dead," as if he'd never seen anyone so dead. I began to bleed from the nose. It was the least I could do.

I was sent to finish high school in a reception centre, where I was to live until I was legally of age. They protected the residents from themselves by covering everything with plastic: furniture, cutlery, food, dreams. I had to endure long sessions with a hyper-emotional social worker that I refused to speak to because I was afraid she would burst into tears. One look was enough for me to guess she was the type of woman who sobs with her bosom heaving, and I had no wish to see her heavy breasts bounce while she listened to my tale of woe. Besides, it would have been indecent to make someone else cry while I had been dry-eyed ever since I'd slipped off my thermal blanket. This wasn't intentional and it certainly was not because I didn't feel sad. But something simply had fallen away from me at the same time as Daniel, and the emptiness that we'd theorized at length together had materialized. A mass of lukewarm air had spread everywhere inside me as though there was nothing left to stop it. Maybe I'd never really wanted to die before the day of our suicide. Maybe it was a bogus idea prompted by our bouts of pessimism, or a game, a kind of posture that made me feel closer to him. But this much is certain: the desire to disappear never let go of me afterward.

I had severed all ties with my foster family and had never developed any relationships other than the one that had crashed at the bottom of the mine, so I had nowhere to go during my weekend leaves. Probably out of habit, as well as guilt, I ended up at the Borduas'. I hadn't seen Daniel's parents since the funeral. That day, they had taken turns collapsing; first his mother had gone to pieces in his father's arms and then she held him when he crumpled like a broken wing. As I knocked on the red door—the key was still lodged in the lining of my jacket—I half hoped the Borduas had converted Daniel's room into a torture chamber where they would make me pay for all those years when they had welcomed me into their home like a poisoned fruit.

Mrs. Borduas opened and her lower lip immediately started to quiver, an insect caught in a net. She screeched,

"Jocelyn!" opening her arms almost brutally to press me against her chest. "We were so worried! We thought they'd locked you up!" Mr. Borduas arrived and he, too, embraced me. I followed them inside. They sat me down in front of a steaming plate and I ate heartily for the first time in weeks. Mrs. Borduas stroked my hair while I blew on each forkful. I had never noticed how much Daniel looked like his mother. The same hesitant eyes, the same undulating head of hair. I lowered my head.

They didn't ask anything or utter a word of reproach, even though they could very well have blamed me for their son's suicide. They were just as kind as they had ever been, even more so in a way. Now there was something piercing in their eyes when they looked at me, as if they were trying to discern in my vague gestures some trace of their son that had survived in me. From then on, I knew I could not die.

I went back to see them every week. They took me in after I left the centre and convinced me to continue my education. This didn't interest me at all, but I remembered how they had dreamed of seeing their son earn a "nice diploma." That's how they referred to everything beyond high school. I enrolled in a CEGEP and eventually graduated as a qualified paramedic. I moved to the city, near the bridge—the Borduas were averse to navigating the clogged arteries of the metropolis—and found work in a hospital. My job involved sterilizing small, razor-sharp instruments and keeping an eye on the equipment and the employees so they wouldn't deploy their army of germs into the rooms where patients were cut open. My tasks were simple and specific, and demanded total concentration. I accepted any overtime that was offered me, day or night, alongside the surliest nurses and the crabbiest doctors. Their barking filled the stale atmosphere of my mind. I would come home from work exhausted and eat slumped in front of the TV. I lived in perennial stasis.

My Sundays were reserved for the Borduas. Sometimes they came for a visit, especially when the sink wouldn't drain or a lamp was on the blink. Mr. Borduas repaired whatever needed repair, keeping up a running commentary on every stage of the operation, and was happy to see me nod whenever he glanced up. Mrs. Borduas brought me little containers of frozen food with the dates and ingredients marked on the lid. Still, despite the long bus ride, I preferred to visit them. They had never sold the house where their son had grown up. Like them, I suppose, I had learned to stop seeing the rooms as boxes full of Daniel's shadows. The place had become a warm, peaceful haven.

Over the years their grief had taken a variety of forms. At first it was raw and prickly, but eventually it mellowed into a kind of smooth sphere that they caressed nostalgically, a healthy but painful habit. The way Daniel's disappearance shaped their daily lives was both horrible and reassuring. And the importance of my presence in maintaining this conflicted balance wasn't lost on me. I had not taken their son's place; I was the instrument that would help them carve out their existence without him, help them skirt around the biggest stumbling blocks while not ignoring them. I believe my face gradually underwent the same process as our bereavement: it grew rounder, its features less distinct. As our grief levelled out, my own attributes fell away and I, too, turned into a bland, reliable, tolerable ball.

I have no hesitation in saying that I love the Borduas, but it was a flat, stagnant sort of love. Like water slumbering at the bottom of a well, but without which you would dry up. I'm certain they loved me with all their heart. I never accomplished anything of note, but they were proud of me. My career was unexceptional, there was no man in my life, motherhood was out of the question, I had no friends. Yet not once did the Borduas remark on my isolation; it seemed that for them just my staying alive was enough of an exploit to nurture their admiration. The wish to die persisted in every breath I took and through each day as it reiterated the day before. I marked time, and my immobility was an impregnable bulwark against suicide.

At the hospital, people I'd worked beside for decades still asked me to repeat my name. Doctors to whom I'd handed hundreds of scalpels acted as though they were seeing me for the first time. Patients whose room I had disinfected in the morning wanted to know in the evening if I was "new here." I'd become imperceptible.

The Borduas slowly grew older. Their skin sagged like the branches of an especially tough plant, their bones became misshapen, yet the smiles that their wrinkles perched on stayed genuine. Watching them, I sometimes caught myself pretending these old folks were Daniel and me, that we'd gotten through our period of reckless sorrows, that I'd made a clean break with the demons of my childhood, and that he had stuffed himself with antidepressants, which I now knew might have done him good. This apparently cozy, unruffled life, this gentle slide toward the last act might have been ours. Even after all that time, I still couldn't decide whether or not I'd have wanted such a life. It was impossible for me to imagine Daniel stable and medicated.

Mr. Borduas was the first to die. A painless embolism in the middle of the night. Mrs. Borduas told me he'd sat up in bed and uttered a few words. Half-awake, she assumed he was talking in his sleep and paid no attention. She had no memory of what he might have said except one word, "Daniel." We buried him in September, and the sun was shining. The sky had never seemed so bright to me.

Mrs. Borduas stayed the same, resilient through her widowhood, her rheumatism, and her prolapse. Two or three times a week, I would cross the bridge and the tired fields of the South Shore to visit her. As I handed her the little frozen dishes that it was my turn now to prepare for her, I marvelled at every detail of the house, which the Borduas had never renovated or modernized. One day, without giving it any thought, I asked her, "You never felt like redecorating? Modern furniture, new curtains? If you like, I could come with you to the store." She gave me a warm-hearted look but shook her head unambiguously. It wasn't necessary for her to spell out what I should have understood long ago. The walls weren't lined with pictures of Daniel. She had discarded his books and notebooks and donated his clothes. She had not transformed her home into a mausoleum, at least, not in an obvious way. It was in the decor, in the permanence of the things among which he had lived, that she paid tribute to him. "Every time you come to see me it's like a breath of fresh air, dear Victoria. I don't need a decorator for that." I felt a wave of melancholy wash over me at the thought that this kind woman would soon be gone.

Less than a year later, Mrs. Borduas was laid low. A stroke forced her to wave a final goodbye to her beloved home, which I promised to take good care of. I went all out to get her admitted to my hospital so I could look after her. I went to see her whenever I had a break and at the end of my shift, and I would sit at her bedside to read to her, help her eat, or simply watch over her while she slept. She liked to fall asleep holding my hand, like a child hoping to fend off the nightmares. She wasn't quite all there, and she often spoke about Daniel as if he were still alive, still the little boy begging for a morsel of biscuit dough or refusing to wash. I didn't contradict her but chose to let her slip freely into those states of confusion, where I supposed she found a kind of peace.

A few days before she died I found her fully awake and alert. The wind was sweeping across the mountain as if to carry off its memories, and I was surprised to find myself wanting to stroll along those poorly marked paths that all led to the same spot. Mrs. Borduas offered me pieces of saltwater taffy that a rare visitor had brought her, fixing her gaze on me more intensely than ever. "Victoria, there's something I'd like to know. Why did our Daniel commit suicide?" She always said "our Daniel," automatically including me in the exclusive club of the people he had belonged to. He was now just a small, very hard point in my mind. But here she was asking the question that had dogged me like Ariadne's thread for all those years. There was still no way to respond. "I don't know, Mrs. Borduas." She wiped away a tear, one of the few I'd seen her shed, and tapped me on the wrist. "And you survived."

I paused momentarily, wavering between the urge to leave unsaid what could never make sense and the feeling that, for once in her life, this woman deserved a truly sincere answer from me. My throat seemed to open on its own. "Yes, I survived. Because I let go of his hand." At this, Mrs. Borduas coughed, something I interpreted as a failure to understand. My body was rigid. "We were supposed to jump together. But I let go of his hand," I repeated. Again, she tapped me on the arm and then closed her eyes. I shuddered from head to foot. I don't know if she learned anything from my confession. Maybe she had guessed long ago that we had been bound by a pact, Daniel and I. Maybe she had suspected it was cowardice that had turned me into a survivor. Maybe my words just dissolved inside her splintered mind.

After a couple of days she began to sink deeper and deeper into a coma. I took a leave of absence; I'm sure my supervisor was surprised to see this stranger apologize for having to take time off. I stayed at Daniel's mother's bedside day and night, wetting her lips, arranging her pillows, wiping her nose and the corners of her eyes, emptying her bedpan without recoiling from the body of the person for whom I'd lived such a useless life. She died a short while ago, silent and calm in the face of the Grim Reaper, quietly waiting for the nurses and residents to leave the room before she expired.

Like the beating wing of a butterfly, her last breath slipped through her lips to seed a storm, a hurricane in the offing. I kissed her on the forehead and went out without letting anyone know. Making my way down the corridors, I passed several colleagues who did not recognize me, even though my hair is combed the same way as always, even though I wear my uniform because I've got nothing else to put on. Even though I'm exactly the same person I was since I slipped my hand out of the grip of the boy I loved.

I step outside and the air is cool. Labrador has reached out with its great squalls, and the gusts lift me from one stair to the next, from asphalt to soft ground. I easily climb a small wooded hill and I feel that the wind will break my bones, open my head and drive out the marshy air, smash me in a headlong plunge onto a pile of granite. But I don't fall; I go up. When I reach the top, the storm is so deafening it covers the ambulance sirens and muffles the horns of drivers hurtling toward a wall or a deer. For once, in the midst of the tumult, the thundering havoc, I'm all right. I lean my back against a tree and have no need for a run up or a rope or a blade. I've waited thirty years, and the end will come naturally, a sudden, spontaneous death.

One, two, three.

"DO YOU RECOGNIZE this woman?"

The tired features, the jaws like a steel frame, the regal hair. Of course, they say. From Quebec City to James Bay, from Gaspé to Nicolet, from Kapuskasing to La Patrie, from Prince Rupert to Niagara, from Miramichi to Slave Lake, from Yellowknife to Rigaud, hundreds have responded to the notice. Of course we know her. She is our grandmother, our sister. She is our neighbour, the mother of our children. She is the woman who taught us how to sew on a button. The one who stuffed us full of bread pudding, who tormented us with all those ghastly cigarette burns. She is the pensioner who slept all the time, who smoked too much, the traveller who came through our village every spring, the parishioner who didn't pay her tithe from 1972 to 1987. She was the first Québécoise I ever kissed. She is the lady I didn't help across the street, and you can see what that led to. She is the woman I had forgotten, that left too soon, that we hoped never to run into again. The one we've been searching for for years. It's for her that we always keep the porch light on now, and no longer turn off our phones, our headlights, our heads. That's her, that's Madame Victoria.

Céleste is a member of the police team tasked with compiling all the calls. She listens to the voicemail messages and notes down names, numbers, and the sometimes scant, sometimes overabundant details provided. First she contacts the ones dubbed "marshmallow cases," the people whose messages suggest they are not in full possession of their mental faculties. Before dismissing their accounts outright she must call everyone back and ask the routine questions. These conversations often take up half her day. It is not easy to cut off someone who is vulnerable, especially if, like Céleste, you wear your heart on your sleeve. If asked for statistics, she would say that forty per cent of marshmallow cases come under the heading of conspiracy theories; they are the most garrulous callers. They can spend two hours trying to convince whoever is listening that Madame Victoria was the victim of some machination of a) the government b) the Church c) a secret society—Freemasons are very popular culprits—or d) alien agents. Though it goes against the grain, Céleste is often obliged to put an abrupt end to such conversations.

Another twenty-five per cent of marshmallow cases are made up of people who, when called back, don't remember having contacted the information line, nor do they have any idea who Madame Victoria might be. Then there are those who give very elaborate accounts that would be credible if they did not end up contradicting themselves, thereby betraying a type of mythomania. These represent fifteen per cent of marshmallow cases and can be quite difficult to unmask. Some ten per cent start berating Céleste as soon as they hear her voice, five per cent cry, and two per cent make lewd propositions. The rest remain a mystery. When she dials the numbers of this enigmatic three per cent, the line has been disconnected or she is told that no one with that name has ever lived there. Such occurrences are too numerous for Céleste to write them off as errors; for her, they are ghosts, witnesses as fugitive as Madame Victoria's identity.

The second half of her day is devoted to the serious calls. These conversations are generally shorter. Céleste registers the places, dates, and all the particulars the caller is able to supply. In the vast majority of cases, the inconsistencies become apparent after only a few questions. Sometimes the time period fits but not the missing woman's age. Sometimes the physical description is promising but not the location. Sometimes people end up admitting it's a child, a man, or a young Haitian girl that they are looking for, but not an older white woman. When Céleste tells them, regretfully, that she must disregard their lead, they insist. Almost all of them, even the ones who obviously have no connection with Madame Victoria, stubbornly put forward far-fetched theories, loudly claiming to have some sort of proprietary right to the nameless woman. Patiently and as gently as possible, Céleste refutes their contentions. No, Victoria did not have a gold tooth. She was not club-footed. She may have had a tattoo with the image of a lynx, but there is no way of knowing. But that wasn't her. It wasn't her.

Initially, Céleste was convinced that uncovering Madame Victoria's life story would be child's play. Yet despite a sound investigation and the countrywide missing person alert, there has been no progress in the case. Céleste is starting to lose hope, and it shows in her exchanges with the callers. They have turned personal. Then, as if by a miracle, an answer arrives. Her name is Léa.

On the telephone, her manner is brusque, as though she had been reluctant to come forward. But the places and dates coincide. She is the right age to be Madame Victoria's daughter. She sends Céleste photos of her mother. Same tired features, same athletic bone structure, same shock of hair as Madame Victoria's. Ever since Léa was a little girl, her mother's life was made up of lean times and wandering. Then, a few months before Madame Victoria's death, she disappeared. Céleste is fired up. She summons Léa to Montreal to run some tests. A hair of the dead woman, a hair of the living woman. Then they wait. During their meetings, the young woman is self-possessed, like someone whose life has just reached an angle of repose after years of turmoil.

In Léa's presence Céleste tries to rein in her excitement, but she can't keep from asking questions; she wants to know everything about the woman who may well be the one everyone is looking for. Léa informs her, though not in so many words, that her mother was bipolar, that she led a nomadic life punctuated by intervals in the psychiatric hospital. Because Léa was placed with a foster family when she was very young, she never lived with her mother and sometimes went for years without seeing her. Céleste would like so much to find a name, a family, a location for Madame Victoria, a resolution that would release her from the silence she is trapped in. Now, however, she also wants to bring some closure to Léa's quest.

The results arrive, and it falls on Céleste to convey them to Léa. The young woman receives the news dispassionately. Taken aback, Céleste reiterates: "I'm sorry, Léa. You're not related to Madame Victoria."

Léa has an obstinate expression as she stares at the wall behind Céleste.

"No," she retorts.

Heavy-hearted, Céleste sets about explaining to her how the DNA tests are carried out, the markers that are examined, the margin of error, the meaning of the results. She repeats that Madame Victoria cannot possibly be her mother or even a distant aunt.

The young woman lifts a flame to the tip of her cigarette. The air catches fire. She blows the smoke skyward, invoking the spirits.

"I don't care. She's still my mother."

Since then, Céleste has stopped distinguishing between the marshmallow cases and the others, the way you stop differentiating, when you reach a certain age, between good and evil, night and day. All these people are asking essentially the same question. How can someone vanish into thin air? How can an arrow never come down again? Victoria belongs to them now. After all, this could be anyone.

Victoria on the Horizon

SHE CAME INTO THE WORLD in an area with a density of seven inhabitants per square kilometre. By the time she reached the legal age, that number had climbed to eight and threatened to continue its appalling ascent. Soon the population of the town on the banks of the Ottawa River would be as dense as woollens washed in hot water. And the proximity of others, whether agglomerated in tight cells or spread out in small solitudes, did not hold the slightest appeal for Victoria or, rather, for her skin. Nearness caused unbearable itching, blotches and blisters, and, in certain extreme cases, a distressing loss of hair. The more people there were around her, the more she scratched.

The affliction struck her on her first day at school. During recess, her skin began to crawl, to rise like an angry sea, producing humours so virulent she felt as if her skin was uttering a thousand cries of pain through its panicked pores. Nearby, the children laughed, sent balls rolling, and drew whole worlds with chalk. Victoria turned her eyes away from her rash, and for an instant a pulse not her own coursed through her body. Then a small group running at full tilt brushed against her and her left side began to burn. She retreated to a deserted corner of the yard and, in a moment of precocious insight, understood that this first fleeting sense of fellowship would be the last. What she had not yet dared to approach she would now be forced to shun.

For three years her mother scrubbed her body with all manner of ointments and witches' salves that irritated Victoria like holy water splashed on demons. In a classroom of forty square metres, the density reached the barbaric ratio of six hundred ninety-four thousand four hundred forty-four people per square kilometre. For Victoria, the significance of the basic demographic unit, the number of people per square kilometre, never diminished; with her gift for mathematics, she assessed each situation in the light of that reassuring measurement. One thing was certain: six hundred ninety-four thousand four hundred forty-four children per square kilometre were far too many for her. When her mother found dried blood on Victoria's sheets and blouses, she resigned herself to homeschooling her daughter.

The years passed and Victoria grew into an uncommonly large young woman, in both height and breadth. Yet she looked hollow, like a mainsail that nothing could fill out. When the time came for her to leave home (forty-five people per square kilometre), Victoria wanted just one thing: to go to the ends of the earth. The joints of her hand were chapped from leafing through atlases and almanacs, her bony fingers caressing the images of the most desolate places in Quebec. She eventually determined that, given its sparse population and majestic landscapes, the tip of the Gaspé Peninsula would make an idyllic spot to settle in. She reasoned that along the coast human density would necessarily feel less burdensome because the expanse of water, which statistics did not factor in, was completely uninhabited.

Thus, she bravely dived into a crammed bus, where she nearly clawed her skin off yet refrained from calculating the number responsible for her suffering. Her neighbour seemed to take mischievous pleasure in jabbing her ribs with his elbow each time he turned the page of his newspaper. When she alighted, she discovered two huge purple blisters at the point of contact. Turning her gaze to the vastness of the sky and sea, she forgot her wounds and heaved a sigh of relief. She was finally far away from everything.

The geese left, taking the summer in tow, the cold came to slow down daily life, the frost varnished the land, and everything stopped. In her small, spare house, Victoria watched in fascination as her skin grew healthy and recovered a creamy purity and smoothness it had not possessed since the cradle. The only human presence was the occasional automobile that entered her field of vision bouncing over the snowy roads too swiftly to send out the wave that corroded every facet and surface of Victoria's body. Standing at the window, she stroked her arms, quietly musing that the only thing life offered her by way of happiness was relief.

To earn a living she did accounting jobs that were delivered by mail. At times, when she took hold of the sheets covered with numbers, her fingers prickled, perturbed by all the agitation, ambitions, and anxieties swarming under the figures she was expected to compile. Then she would let the documents sit for a few hours in the radiance of the wood stove before taking them up again. When she had finished her work she was stiff with a distant fatigue, deliciously different from the exhaustion brought on by her erstwhile ailments. She would wait until the middle of the night to go out and slip the envelopes into the mailbox, certain that at that hour she would encounter nothing but big winds.

Convinced she was saved, Victoria was unsuspecting when the snow began to disappear, the ice jams shrank, the boats once more set out to sea, and the townspeople took possession of the village again. Their distant, hazy presence, their restrained gestures, and their continual migration to the cities prevented them from destabilizing her new-found health. Nor did she fret when the road traffic increased, speckling the landscape with gleaming colours. It was her skin that sounded the alarm in the dead of night during the Saint-Jean holiday. She thought her sheets had caught fire.

There they were, all around her, on the waterfront, in the woods, atop the cliffs and near the rushing stream, drunk and famished, tangled up in their sleeping bags, their mouths brimming with bawdy songs and shrimp, full of the benighted enthusiasm so typical of tourists the world over. At dawn, armed with binoculars, Victoria managed to catch sight of the banners signalling the festivities that would last until autumn. Looking down, she gazed at the festering sores that in a matter of hours had broken out on her chest. Even her nails bristled with scales.

She tried rubbing herself with the old ointments, to no avail; they evaporated upon contact with her skin. Immersed in her bath, she spent a few hours attempting to regain her composure, hoping this unprecedented bout was just a relapse due to a prolonged hiatus. But to her great dismay the water began to seethe and then turn a distressing ochre colour. She leaped out of the bathtub, flayed alive, her vision clouded over by something she sensed was not a product of the ambient air but her own retinas. Twenty-four hours after the vacationers had arrived, Victoria feared for her life.

In no time, her bags were packed. She crossed the sleeping village under cover of early dawn, enraged at being dispossessed of the ground she had gained at such great cost. After a boat ride almost as taxing as the bus ride that had preceded it, Victoria dashed to a quiet, isolated spot to study her map. This time there were no calculations. She knew precisely where she had to go. It was a place that, ironically, was made almost uninhabitable by the swarms of mosquitoes, deer flies, and biting midges, which was why Victoria had previously dismissed it. But realizing now that human proximity was more harmful to her than these insects, she immediately set out in that direction with no second thoughts. She was an arrow, and she was flying toward northern Quebec.

Walking at a brisk pace she could cover twenty-five kilometres a day. In other words, two weeks as the crow flies. But considering the detours needed to avoid the occasional dwellings along the way, she could hardly hope to reach her destination in less than twenty days. She left behind the coastal hamlets and entered what the locals called the "unorganized territory," a wild and marvellously unpopulated expanse stretching from the river to the pole. The only creatures she came across were sufficiently afraid of her to keep their distance. In any case, Victoria had always been more comfortable with the closeness of animals than that of human beings. She therefore allowed herself to break her stride to admire the hefty grace of a moose or the rhythm of a hare in full flight.

Her stigmas faded together with the impression of consuming the air around her. Her skin remained dry and slack, as though her body was a smaller version of an even bulkier physique. But Victoria had never concerned herself with her appearance, which was far less a matter of image than of sensation, and now that she was shooting toward the horizon like a stray bullet, it no longer mattered at all.

She came across scattered objects, gutted machines and stillborn tools, strewn along a deserted road. When she began to notice flowers sprouting in the middle of the pavement she realized she had reached what she was looking for. A density of 0.1 inhabitants per square kilometre. That perfectly smooth zero, burnished by tranquility and seclusion, was her salvation. The vestiges of human activity kept showing up like fallen satellites until Victoria spotted a sign: *Site de l'ancienne ville de Gagnon*, the site of the former city of Gagnon. She had arrived.

Nothing was left of the municipality except the washed-out pattern of the streets. The houses, the school, the church, the stores—everything had been flattened when the company pulled out. On the outskirts of the city, sitting in a pool of toxic water at the bottom of a massive hole, were the machines the managers of the mine had not seen fit to take with them. Metallic fossils, scorified whale skeletons. Witnessing this scene of dereliction, Victoria discovered what all undertakers come to terms with through their acquaintance with corpses: the grey, unalterable peace of death. She moved through a kind of silvery desert coldly glimmering with deposits of a heavy, bluish powder. They had extracted from the belly of the earth whatever was needed to turn this part of the country into a moonscape. The wind came up and the smell of the tundra brushed against her bare skin. Nature, so beautiful, so volatile.

She spent several days sleeping outdoors, with the bats weaving protective trails overhead. In the absence of other humans, her solitude took on a new texture. Whereas before she had to fight to build an invisible bubble around her, in Gagnon such efforts were no longer necessary. The struggle was quite simply to survive. She had brought only a thick sleeping bag and dehydrated food that she ate sparingly. In the creeks and the immense arms of the Manicouagan reservoir she caught fish that kept on battling until the moment of death, and coming into contact with their vitality made her tremble. She was unaccustomed to it. She prepared and cooked her prey with reverence.

In August the weather took an uncertain turn and shelter became a pressing need. Victoria took up residence in a place bordered by magnificent aspens, where, she assumed, a very cozy house had once stood. To find the necessary materials she had to move away from the centre of town, which had been stripped decades ago. Sometimes she walked up to twenty kilometres a day to locate a few planks, branches suitable for supporting a structure, some sheet metal. She erected a cabin with what she found and insulated it with leaves and moss. It felt good to build her nest where people had lived, loved, lied, wept, where men had bled and women had swaddled babies. The days grew shorter and she began to gather firewood. She stole sheets and canned goods as heavy as bear bellies from the seldom-used hunting lodges of Lac Barbel.

These preparations plunged her into a kind of frenzy. She started talking to herself and to the fallen leaves, the squirrels, the last moths. She told herself legends inspired by the strange topography of this city reclaimed by nature, and confided in its inhabitants, whose souls had not entirely gone away. Submerged since her early childhood, the desire for human contact resurfaced, compounded by the looming season of hardships. From the traces of warmth and friendship that surrounded her, she invented the warmth and friendship she lacked. Then the first snows settled on her new kingdom and she fell silent.

Those who have experienced real pain, the kind of torment that claws at the outer limits of what a person can endure, understand what a blessing immobility can be. After years of suffering, Victoria bore with equanimity the need to stay huddled in a shelter so narrow that she was forced to sleep curled up, to eat in a squatting position, to let her thoughts go round in circles. During the blizzards, she sat perfectly still inside her shell of stiff cloth, feeling that winter had stuffed her in its pocket like an old glove. Even though the fire produced enough heat to keep her alive, the big freezes numbed her extremities and a perilous sleep tormented her on more than one night, as the wolves awakened around her.

Yet the danger of freezing and the wild beasts might have been kept at bay if hunger had not gained ground, slithering through the snow like an endless snake. Because when it becomes permanent, hunger eventually is forgotten, and therein lies the danger. The supply of canned food and dry cereals that had appeared substantial in the fall depleted very quickly, and the frugal rations that Victoria afforded herself were dispersed inside her as soon as they were swallowed. With her skin immaculate as never before, she counted the days until the thaw, making delirious calculations in which her exhaustion served as the numerator and winter, the denominator. By the time spring came gliding across the incalculable planet of the north, Victoria had been devoured by the winds and the solitude of the Manicouagan. Like the city where she had taken up residence, she was now just a phantom.

She was aware that on the first day of warm weather she crawled out of her lair, lapped up meltwater, and caught sight of some geese, which she wished she could roast. She later would recall raising her head to receive the boreal forest and its shower of luminous needles, the greedy mouth of spring. She blacked out somewhere between her triumph over the season of death and the failure of her calculations. Under the expanding sun her skin grew iridescent. The sound of footsteps ruffled the silence.

From the depths of her coma she felt her malady returning. It started with a prickly sensation, followed by outright itching, which, given her paralysis, she could not relieve. The torture lasted several hours, during which she inferred from the jolts and jerks that she was being transported elsewhere. A specific point between her breasts began to burn with unusual intensity, and Victoria grasped through some feverish intuition that she had arrived at the place she had never dared to go. Through her pain she was overtaken by a weird joy, a savage jubilation born of transgression, the abandonment of all her efforts. She found herself thrown against others, packed, moulded into the crowd. She was saved. She was damned.

When she awoke there was a syringe in her arm and a nurse slathering her body with a petroleum-based cream. "Don't bother," Victoria managed to mutter as she eyed the huge blisters that covered her skin. The nurse jumped. Doctors hurried to her room to take samples of her skin while Victoria swallowed pills that did nothing to dull her pain. Only a step away from downtown Montreal, the population density exceeded three thousand per square kilometre. Within the walls of the Royal Victoria Hospital that number increased tenfold. Analgesics were powerless to deal with this degree of human concentration.

While she was being fed, intravenously at first and then with small meals as pale as the rain, she learned that six days earlier a hunter had found her in the woods exhausted and severely undernourished. He had immediately driven her to this hospital without explaining why he hadn't left her in Baie-Comeau, La Malbaie, or Quebec City. Dizzy with pain, Victoria barely managed to follow the nurse aides' account. For hours at a time she crunched ice cubes and looked out the window at the men and women jostling each other on the overcrowded sidewalks, delighted and horrified by this unthinkable proximity.

When she was able to walk and eat unaided, she got out of her bed. Her skin was covered with sores, even her feet floated on a layer of gigantic blisters; the staff was against her going out. Victoria shook her head, touched by the kindness of all these people with their drawn faces, their prominent cheekbones, their almond eyes, their laughing mouths, their protruding ears. She never grew tired of seeing this multitude of faces. She promised to come back every day for the treatment that was supposed to cure her and left.

She could walk no more than ten metres without halting, staggered by a pain so acute it blinded her. But she did not have far to go. From her room she had noticed a small, isolated wood overlooking the parking lot. It would do. This knoll would allow her to establish a buffer zone within a radius of thirty metres around her. Considering the density to which she had become accustomed over the past weeks, this perimeter would afford her some respite. Besides, she could not walk any farther.

She fashioned a small nest of leaves and, rocked by the sirens and the music of the evening, she spent a tolerable first night. She had not been mistaken. The moderate isolation eased her suffering. In the morning she hobbled back to the hospital to receive her medication and undergo tests. The medical staff seemed to have run out of solutions but they persisted in believing something on the fringe of their science could help their flayed patient. This perseverance made them even more endearing.

On Victoria's fifth day in the wood, a chubby nurse no taller than a rosebush led her into an office and shut the door. "I know you're sleeping in the parking lot. I could help you find a place to stay, you know," she said, riveting her eyes of different colours on those of her patient. Victoria shrugged: "I don't sleep in the parking lot, I sleep in the wood. Please don't be offended, but the time I spend there does me far more good than the medicines you give me." She described to the lady the things she had done over the past few years to fight her strange allergy. "Then why don't you go back to the countryside?" Victoria smiled and felt the crusts on her face go taut. "I don't know," she answered, unable to explain that she could no longer detach herself from the crowd that made her ill.

That evening, the woman insisted on accompanying Victoria to the top of the knoll. She placed a blanket and a package of food near the makeshift bed. "Sleep well. See you tomorrow." In a sudden surge of affection, Victoria took a step forward and wrapped her arms around the nurse, who compassionately returned the embrace and even bestowed a few exquisite taps on Victoria's shoulder. As the nurse made her way back down to the hospital, Victoria, shaken by the hug, began to tremble.

In the middle of her breastbone, the point of tension that had been radiating heat since her arrival in Montreal expanded. A searing pain invaded her chest, her trunk, her neck, and finally her head. Her skin simmered like water about to evaporate. She wanted to scream but all she could manage was a hoarse wheeze. Her body was burning. In a panic she threw herself down and rolled on the ground. The carpet of dead leaves ignited.

On Mount Royal, the dogs sniffed the air. A smell of incense, wintergreen, and scorched spruce floated through the trees. A tender-hearted Great Dane began to howl; a flock of birds scattered in the plume of smoke rising from the slope of the mountain. Without knowing why, people strolling along there suddenly felt like crying.

Victoria Worn Out

SOMEWHERE BETWEEN the eleventh and the twelfth she'd had enough. It had already set in with the eighth, the fraught, irreparable tiredness, when nights brought her dreams where her arms came loose and dropped to the ground with a soft thud. Then she became pregnant with her ninth, and her sleep turned back into the thick substance that engulfed everything and made her snore. But when the third wife announced with tears of joy in her heifer eyes that she was expecting twins, Victoria decided it was time to get out.

The first wife gave up after her fourth child and never leaves her bed now despite the prayers, despite the songs sung for her by the matrons of the community. Victoria was entrusted with her offspring, so that from one day to the next her brood doubled in size. She ate incessantly in those days, seeking in the meat pies and crusty breads the energy that drained out of her each time she nursed, each time she awoke in the night. After that, she resigned herself to being thin. Nothing can satiate her, neither food nor faith.

The small white bodies that surround her are interchangeable, just like the names of these sons and daughters all demanding to be washed, warmed, fed, consoled, taught to walk and speak, tucked into bed, and cared for when they come down with the runny noses, chesty coughs, and stomach viruses that befall the household like disasters. The husband doesn't consider it incumbent on him to help out, and the third wife has always believed she does her fair share by singing lullabies and making necklaces out of macaroni.

So Vanda is mixed up with Nephi, who becomes Justicia or Laerte when it's time for homework or Noah during a snowstorm. At bath time, all these little slippery-skinned creatures follow each other through the bathwater, which gradually turns brown, while Victoria, getting damper and damper, feels her hands shrivel up and eventually steps out of the bathroom dripping wet. She ought to find the children's laughter and words endearing, but they're smothered by the screen of her exhaustion before reaching her ears. She gives them each a kiss and aligns their small bodies in overcrowded beds, pulls up the quilts, and turns off the light the way one hastily shuts a door to keep out the cold.

The kids' uncertain sleep signals the beginning of new tasks where their shadows continue to haunt the house. The bits of food glued under the table. The evaporated drops of pee around the toilet bowl. The clothes discarded in the corners of the rooms. The thousands of toys pulled as if by magnets underneath the sofas. The nose pickings stuck to the back cover of the Book of Mormon. The dying animals hidden in the basement in the hope of saving their lives and which, if not found in time, will fill the house with a stench of putrefaction. Then, after the housecleaning, the laundry, the sewing, and the next day's sandwiches, there are the prayers. To give thanks for the boon that a large family represents.

She lives in the southwestern part of the continent; she sets course for the northeast. With its catastrophic climate and its reputation as a Sodom, Montreal is the last place they'll look for her. Victoria packs in secret, one article at a time, more when the husband spends the night with the third wife, but such occasions have grown scarcer as number three's belly grows larger. Victoria crams an assortment of essential items into her suitcase, doing her utmost to assemble whatever clothing and material is needed to prepare for what awaits her in that city of snow and promiscuity. Whenever a child coughs or farts in the next room she quickly shuts the suitcase, her heart racing. They sleep restlessly, unable to stop fidgeting, to stop making their tenacious little presence felt.

The main problem is money. When the husband is away, she is the one who holds the purse strings. But a theft would very soon be noticed, easily sniffed out in this household so mindful of its budget, so devoted to scrimping and saving. And it's out of the question for Victoria to spend years building up a nest egg by skimming small change from the kitty on the sly. She needs a more radical method to finance her getaway. She considers raiding the temple's cashbox but is too afraid of the consequences. The community does not take that sort of offence lightly.

The solution comes to her one feverish night as she surveys the assembly to whom she has just served the sacred stew. Casting her eyes on the eldest son, a blond-haired lad prophetically named Croesus, she realizes he has been delivering papers for quite a while. Come to think of it, she can't remember a time when Croesus didn't spend his mornings seated astride his dilapidated bicycle distributing vapid publications rolled up like scrolls. Searching her memory, she recalls that on several occasions the boy voiced the desire to donate to the Church's African missions. First thing the next day, she snatches her son's piggybank. Just as she hoped, the delicate porcelain piglet contains enough money for her to cross the continent and subsist for two or three weeks. Victoria seizes the loot with no second thoughts. The infidels of Africa can wait. Her own impiety is a matter of urgency.

The larceny sets things in motion. Checking the bus schedules, the routes, the times when the coast would be clear. Thrusting her hand under the bed in the middle of the night to be reassured by the touch of the suitcase handle. Shouldering the husband's body away when he rolls toward her. Above all, avoiding pregnancy. Especially now. On every surface, disorder is on the rise, and the children have begun to swear under their breaths, as if the house sensed the imminent chaos. In her head she is already far. She is an arrow that nothing can divert from its flight north.

She chooses to leave the day after the Sabbath. Sleep is more impenetrable on those nights and the early morning heavier. Cousins have come to the house to celebrate, and the floors are littered with bodies slumbering on camping mattresses, dressed in blue, pink, and a dirty white now beyond washing. She can't distinguish her sons and daughters among the pug-nosed faces. They all look alike. The children of her family have become one child, a single little person uttering an inarticulate request, an impossible prayer, with one voice. One pair of legs cavorting back and forth along the corridor, one head of hair beset by chewing gum.

Victoria threads her way through the sleepers, careful not to brush them with her long skirt. The door creaks when she opens it, and a little girl with a tousled mane lifts her head, scratches her behind, wipes her nose with the sleeve of her nightgown. Victoria raises a finger to her lips to hush the child. Then she steps through the doorway with a sigh that carries her to the far end of the deserted street, to the station full of birds and prayer sheets. Others have gone adrift here before her.

During the endless bus ride, Victoria recalls the horror stories brought back by the young missionaries returning from Montreal. The bars where women dance and hike up their skirts like Jezebels, vagrants who bite people going by, alcoholics who drink themselves to death, temples converted into condominiums. Not that she's unable to credit these accounts, but they don't shock her anymore. The time when she believed that those who left the trenches of the Church fell into an abyss is long past. Now she is one of the so-called "sons of perdition," and she doesn't care. The last circle of the Mormon hell is better than that community and its stifling rules. No dancing. No lottery tickets. No hot beverages. No refusing the husband's body. The first thing she'll do after getting off in Montreal will be to drink a cup of coffee hotter than the sun and scratch a lottery ticket while doing a few tango steps.

The weather is fine when she arrives in Montreal. It's milder than she expected, but Victoria insists on wearing a heavy parka. She takes a seedy room next to the bus station, puts down her luggage, chucks the Bible that was asleep in the night table, and finally lies down. It seems to her, on this bed with lumpy blankets, that this is the first time she has ever stretched out. Except for her deliveries, she has never spent this much time both awake and horizontal. Nor has the silence around her ever been so perfect. The noise of the engines and the horns rising from the street is nothing compared to the fleshy thrum that set the tempo of her former life and nurtured the feeling that at any moment someone might show up, tug at her arm and demand of her a thousand things meant to remedy the inexorable fact that whatever you fill will eventually be empty again, whatever you heal will end up hurting again, whatever you satisfy will sooner or later be unappeased. She falls asleep.

After forty-eight hours of dizzying stillness Victoria resolves to confront the outside world. The roads are grey and grimy, and wet in spite of the dry weather; the people are old and tetchy and refuse to look at her. She could not have wished for anything better. She goes to watch the river and the ships, passes in front of dozens of churches without paying attention, and hikes up the mountain. Everything is constantly moving and, oddly enough, this movement, with which she has no connection, calms her. Montreal is precarious and full of gaps; fitting in will be easy. Everything will be easier, from now on.

She devotes the following week to job hunting, making the rounds of the shops, supermarkets, and fast-food restaurants, offering her services as a cashier. After all those years managing the family budget, her mental arithmetic skills are unrivalled, and the prospect of establishing a border of numbers and banknotes between her and her peers appeals to her. Wherever she applies, she is appraised with a stern look, sometimes her telephone number is noted down, but she senses from the vague gestures with which she is received that the moment she turns around her particulars will wind up at the bottom of a wastebasket. She has no résumé, no references, not even a fixed address. No one wants to hire a ghost.

One afternoon she finds herself in front of a pizzeria. To save money, she has been making do until now by nibbling on white bread and a few thin slices of ham. But after the long days spent marching from one neighbourhood to the next in search of work, she hungers for something hot, fat, and heavy. Liberated at last from the greed of gluttonous children, she wants to chomp on her favourite foods and hear the smack of her selfishness between two mouthfuls. She enters the eatery, ready to sacrifice a portion of her savings, which life in the big city has depleted faster than she'd expected.

At the counter, a waitress with hair as frizzy as a lamb is serving customers in three broken languages. Behind her, an oil-soaked sign announces that the restaurant is hiring. She glances at the greenish walls and squeaky stools, and pictures herself carrying plates of Caesar salad and garlic bread. Victoria intercepts the waitress as she walks by, introduces herself and enquires about the job offer. Showing no interest in Victoria's waitressing skills, the woman asks if she speaks French.

"I have to speak French?!" Victoria exclaims.

Clicking her tongue in a show of resignation, the waitress says in an English tinged with Italian, "You'll never find a job if you don't speak both languages. What did you do before?"

"Well, I took care of children."

The woman's face is transformed, like the facade of a building where all the shutters have just swung open simultaneously. Looking decisive, the lamb pulls a sheet of notepaper from her back pocket and scribbles something down.

"It's my sister's number. She's looking for someone. Call her."

Victoria stuffs the paper into her handbag. A half-hour later she has her first appointment for a job interview. She had not been mistaken. This faithless, lacklustre metropolis is just the right place for her. She returns to her hotel with a cheerful spring in her step.

The woman who greets her the day of the interview could hardly have denied her kinship with the waitress at the pizzeria. Younger, plumper, she has the same helmet of densely curled hair. But unlike her brown-eyed sister, she is odd-eyed. It's disconcerting.

Madame Eon ushers Victoria into her house, which is fitted out in a peculiar way. On one side are a bedroom and a kitchen redolent with the usual smells of a North

American home: beer, red meat, and disappointment. The other side is marked off by low gates and painted in colours so bright they hurt Victoria's eyes. The walls are covered with clumsy attempts at representing animals, houses, and other nondescript objects, all fashioned by unskilled minds. The odour given off by this part of the residence is unmistakable: the place is regularly invaded by children, young children. Even if she pinched her nostrils shut, Victoria could detect the smell of milk and loaded diapers.

Madame Eon confirms her visitor's diagnosis.

"I run a family child-care centre. My clientele is Anglophone or allophone. My assistant quit on me this week. With twelve kids, including infants, I need at least two educators to satisfy the government's ratio requirements. Even though this is not a subsidized service I have to meet the standards, you understand?"

Ignoring the obscure jargon used by the woman, Victoria scans the place. Miniature chairs. Bins full of toys gnawed by burgeoning teeth. Dog-eared books. Potties, one blue, one pink, with their crowns of bacteria. Cribs. She shakes her head.

"It's not the kind of work I had in mind."

Madame Eon gives her an imploring look.

"I can't," Victoria insists.

But inside her too roomy pocket, her fingers start to twitch. In five days she'll have nothing left to pay for her modest room. Her recent extravagance has not made her stupid; she has little chance of finding another job before then. "This could tide me over," she tells herself as she kicks away a ball that has rolled up to her big toe. She looks directly into Madame Eon's blue eye—or is it green?—and shakes her hand. Right then she feels something sting her neck and flattens the palm of her free hand against her carotid artery. She pulls her hand away and examines it. Nothing. An invisible insect.

Her first shift turns into a succession of days that flow one into the next so seamlessly that what was supposed to be temporary soon becomes an immutable cycle from which, inexplicably, she can't escape. If she had the leisure to mull it over she might conclude it was predestined or the work of some manipulative, vengeful gods, a kind of enslavement to her fate. But she doesn't have the time to indulge in such musings.

Madame Eon's day-care centre is at once organized and untamed. The day is divided along lines that, theoretically, are very clear but are blurred by crying jags, allergy attacks, and snot. Thus, despite the schedule for naps, the young residents rarely sleep at the same time. Meals never really end; the instant a snack is over, the table is reloaded with food as soft and white as the clay out of which these munching creatures have been moulded. No sooner has Victoria finished serving than diapers get filled up, and the older children's urgent needs multiply at a furious rate amid a commotion of wailing and accidents in pants already soiled from previous mishaps.

The paint intended for motor and creative development ends up on the clothes and in the mouths of the youngest. An educational toy with rounded edges reveals, a split second too late, a blunt corner that inflicts bruises as deep blue as the sea, which Victoria quickly conceals with plasters. As the end of the day approaches and Victoria worries about handing over to the always-in-a-hurry parents a bunch of kids covered in gouache and bandages, the kids miraculously transform into clean, undamaged little beings.

But the absence of children never lasts more than a few minutes. Through some inscrutable process, the quiet moments disintegrate as soon as they arise, and new children come to replace the old ones. The fact is that Madame Eon, who dreams of astronomical profits, has decided to keep the doors of her establishment open on weekends and evenings to accommodate parents with atypical schedules or who put a premium on social events. As a result, the day-care centre is crowded with tots at all hours of the day and night, and Victoria, unable to extricate herself from the seething syrup of early childhood, spends weeks of continual wakefulness wiping gummy fingers and keeping kids from falling into sinks full of soaking dishes that never quite get cleaned.

She couldn't say which is more exhausting: the perpetual recommencement of maternity of her previous life or the never-ending return of different children in Madame Eon's place. In any case, this, too, is beyond the realm of the things she has the luxury of pondering. Just as she's given up trying to understand how human beings this stupid can grow up so fast, she has also stopped examining herself, questioning herself, and analyzing her ailments and her tiredness. Of course, she feels her muscles stretching until they're just limp cords, her arms afflicted with tics and spasms. She feels her knees popping each time she lifts an overweight baby—they're all overweight, fed as they are on goose fat and starch. But whereas she had reflected on her situation back home and concluded she must leave, here, the whirlwind of chores and emergencies keeps her from withdrawing from her environment even for a second, and she slowly sinks into this routine, where the yearnings that she brought to Montreal dissolve one by one.

She gets the feeling every now and then that time has remained suspended since the first day she entered this house and that whole generations have passed through her hands, where they were rocked and wiped before racing toward adulthood; that, in their turn, those adults, the corners of their mouths still studded with cereal crumbs, send her their offspring not yet able to speak their given names; that from one generation to the next these people are increasingly shapeless, and that in a few years nothing will be left of them but vague outlines.

At other moments, however, it seems to her she arrived just yesterday and that time in fact has stretched so that each second has opened up and let in thousands of minuscule instants inhabited by microscopic pains. Because despite all their awkwardness and idiocy, children, especially those in Madame Eon's house, are capable of the coldest acts of cruelty. Tiny knives concealed under a good layer of fat and filth.

Take, for instance, her broken nails, which she initially put down to accidents; Victoria soon realizes it was the children, with their plastic cutlery and wooden hammers, that have been crushing her fingertips. At play, they butt her with their heads, apparently unintentionally, leaving her with bruises and a bitten tongue. It takes her a little while to notice the kids' sideways glances after these misdemeanours, their looks of satisfaction, even amusement on seeing the blood trickle down their keeper's chin.

On her legs and stomach she discovers burns as long as whips. She has no recollection of what might have caused these wounds. True, there's always hot milk sitting on the counter, and boiling water to cook eggs in, and a generic sauce simmering on the stove. But are the children really capable of handling these things without hurting themselves? She doesn't believe it, but when she catches some of them avidly eyeing her blisters she's not so sure anymore. Unable to make up her mind, all she can do is mop the table with a fetid rag to erase the splatters of strawberry jam. It's the kids she would like to wipe away with her dishcloth.

One day, as she's going down to the basement to store some damaged toys, the door slams shut behind her and sends her tumbling to the bottom of the stairs, where she ends up with a badly sprained ankle. This time there's no room left for doubt. Peals of high-pitched laughter ring out on the other side of the door. Victoria hobbles back up the stairs as quickly as she can to unmask the culprits. But there is no one behind the door. From the dormitory comes the sound of reedy snoring. The noise of a remote-controlled model airplane buzzes out under a door. Madame Eon convinces her that a little ice and a rudimentary bandage will suffice to fix her ankle; Victoria obediently returns to the yoke of her duties.

But the incidents don't end there. Growing less timid and more brazen, the children start to attack her more openly. They hit her with sticks when she least expects it, pinch her under cover of darkness, bite her the way one crunches a juicy apple. And the more they hound her, the less able Victoria is to punish the nasty beasts, to respond to a cruelty that appears to be both unconscious and calculated. The ambiguity of childhood paralyzes her. Madame Eon, constantly busy counting her money and putting up a good show for the parents, is completely oblivious, and Victoria would rather die than admit her inability to defend herself against such petty little monsters.

Even the ones she thought were the gentlest manage to hurt her. A sly caress creeps around to her back and leaves a claw-like slash. An eager hug ends up choking her and she must struggle to break free of the stranglehold. At times, when she is exhausted, Victoria takes the liberty of sitting down and closing her eyes. She awakes to find her thumbnail has been completely torn off, that a patch of her hair is missing, that there's a bluish half-moon shining above her eye. The wounds heal, but the erosion of her body worsens. The rebellion that had driven her to leave the world where she was once captive withers away. The more she works, the weaker she grows; the weaker she grows, the more the work becomes an obligation, an inescapable fact, an upper-case verb.

She will never know what put an end to this cycle. One morning, she opens her eyes. She is stretched out in the middle of the corridor. There is silence all around; her whole body cries out in pain. She shivers as she raises her head. The house seems empty, something inconceivable. She calls out; her call drops back down like a dead pigeon. Sitting up, she realizes she is lying in a pool of blood. The sticky fluid appears concentrated, condensed, as though it had refrained from spreading for fear of being sucked up by a young vampire. She lifts her shirt. She wears the same shirt every day. She was probably wearing this shirt the day she declined and then accepted the job Madame Eon was offering her. Her stomach is riddled with deep holes where something seems to be smouldering. On the walls there are paler splashes of blood, possibly someone else's, or her own, diluted by fatigue. By the rush of a battle. By a dash toward freedom.

Summoning up all her strength, she gets to her feet. In front of her, the door is banging in the wind, letting in gusts of winter, keen and glaring. Who could have neglected to close it? Who are the runaways or the intruders she allowed in, or out? Victoria looks around. Everything, every sound, is motionless, petrified. She feverishly steps toward the exit, certain that she is dreaming, until her feet land on the porch and thousands of shards of ice pierce the mesh of her slippers. The shock of the cold seizes her; she straightens up and totters toward the street.

The snow is blinding. Victoria has not really seen the winter since arriving in Montreal, only its traces: damp mittens, brown puddles in the front hall, fractures produced by the collision of ice and bones. She lurches forward as though, deep inside her, a lever had snapped. Yet she manages to reach the street and, impelled by some burning certainty, she heads east. Walking slowly, she traverses the city blocks, trailing behind her a delicate red thread. The quiet neighbourhoods give way to busy thoroughfares. Ambulances speed past, telling her she is going in the right direction. A number of times her vision blurs and spasms crumple her stomach.

She can't remember her last meal. Come to think of it, she's not sure she has really eaten during all those years (or was it days? months? decades?) working for Madame Eon. But she isn't hungry; she is sleepy. In the distance a promising "H" shines in the icy sun.

When she arrives at the gate, her heart lifts. As she enters the hospital grounds, she feels calm. Her aches and failures are less painful, her blood pumps more slowly. The old trees protect her; the building's grey stones whisper soothing words. She needs to reach a door, one of the dozens of doors that beckon her, and go into this place where she can lie down at last. Entrust her broken body to others and be helped by other people without making the slightest effort in return.

But halfway there she stops short. On the till-now virgin snow, footprints appear. Very small footprints that descend toward her and stop, abruptly, right there, in front of her own poorly shod feet. Her heart jumps, the cold catches up with her. She looks around in disbelief, looks through the bushes on the edge of the parking lot, then up and, once again, behind her. The tracks of children's boots are unmistakable, as though cut out by a hole punch. She frantically skirts around the footprints, fixes her eyes on the hospital, and quickens her pace. But she soon comes upon another set of footprints. Once again, the invisible feet seem to have outflanked her and then closed in to more easily climb up her spine. Terrified, Victoria changes direction. She scurries toward the mountain.

With each stride the warmth of the hospital recedes and the woods grow denser. She thinks she sees apples gleaming on a fruit tree, the surface of a lake through the branches and trunks. She hears what sounds like laughter, the howl of a coyote. Now she no longer sees anything but her legs sinking into the snow, this immaculate snow imprinted with so many secrets, passages, escapes, and pursuits. This snow that refuses to melt when touched by her bare hand—or perhaps her own skin is dissolving in the snowflakes? The mountain has begun to cast its shadow over the city.

What the missionaries omitted from the accounts of their voyages was the appeal of winter. The serene way of calling you, snagging you in its raw mesh. The subsequent lethargy, the burning and the shivering, the letting go. As Victoria advances, the frost erases her mind, annihilates her strength. When she falls to her knees she understands that her true destination was neither the north nor childhood. It was the cold.

She struggles, mustering her inner fevers. The bite turns into heat, an irresistible ignition; she could undress, right there in the polar wind, but she lacks the strength. Her wound has almost stopped bleeding. There will be no stain, no mark to signal her presence. Rustling sounds reach her, move toward her, then fade away. Nursery rhymes zigzag among the trees. She would like to stop up her ears, grab onto a memory, perhaps her own childhood, far away and inexplicable, to obliterate all the childhoods that devoured her other ages. But her head grows white, her arms and mind sink once again. Amid the numbness of her body, only her eyes testify to her last wish. A moment of her own.

Victoria in Love

FIRST, I LIGHT A FIRE. There's always sufficient dry wood; I'm the one who goes to fetch it in the evening so it can dry overnight. I like to stack the logs and fit them together just so, with the bark turned skyward. I like to run my thumb over the patterns etched on them and afterwards to sniff my finger. The scent is always the same, at once young and old, sap and fungus.

Then I put the water on to boil. The two big kettles ring like church bells when I fill them up. One kettleful will serve to make tea for Madame, a thick soup, hard-boiled eggs, and to wash the dishes. With the other I'll do the laundry, using the soap that burns your hands. Every day I soak the sheets, shirts, underpants, handkerchiefs, rags, and bonnets. Saturday, I wash my own clothes, to get them clean for Mass. My petticoats are riddled with a thousand tiny holes that make pictures no one else can see.

After the water comes the bread baking. I knead the dough and let it sit through the night; next morning I just have to slip that pretty ball inside the oven's mouth. But first I press my forefinger down on it, and when I lift my finger I feel the mass of dough wanting to follow, to float up to me like a chubby angel. I pray for the bread to rise well. It's a childhood habit—I was flogged whenever I botched the bread. That was during the war.

The sun comes up; Madame rings. I climb the stairs to her bedroom and let the light in, prop up her pillows, serve her tea. She'll have her bread and eggs later, downstairs. She's copied this routine from the English. I still don't understand which things are fit to be copied from the English and which ought not to be shared with them, so I never talk about it. I empty Madame's chamber pot. Sometimes there's blood, but less and less. I like the smell of blood. It reminds me of my mother.

Bertaud, the hired man, arrives early and I serve him his porridge. He can't speak. He's big as an ox and his breath smells of melted snow. His voice and thoughts go astray in that large, cavernous body of his and they never get out. Madame says the doctor dropped Bertaud on his head while pulling him out of his mother's womb, and it's kept him simple. I'm quite fond of him, myself. He's strong and kind and regards everyone with the same fearful gentleness. He draws no distinction between masters and slaves, just as he can't tell the difference between dogs and foxes.

Once breakfast is done and Madame has dressed, while the laundry is soaking and the soup is on the simmer, I clean house. Broom, feather duster, brush, rag; bedrooms (thoroughly), boudoir (carefully), library (quickly), dining room (vigorously). In winter, the slush marks in the front hall must be removed. Whatever the season, I must clean the manure off the doorsill because Madame can't stand the house smelling of the mare. When I was little we used dung to caulk our cabin. That was when we were runaways, before Mama died and Monsieur bought me for a barrel of gunpowder. It was wartime. Horse turds saved my life.

In the afternoon, Madame lies down and the silence smothers the house like a big hunk of bread in a small mouth. Greta—she worked here before me—called it "headache time." Greta got sold to a mitten manufacturer because she knitted better than anyone and was constantly talking back to Madame. To me headache time means going to market. I slip on a pair of fingerless gloves so I can feel the coins in my pocket, the firmness of the apples, the satin of the air. I hurry over to Place Royale, where I meet Augustine, who always has a piece of sugar for me, wrapped and concealed in her half-toothless mouth. They count every grain of sugar at Madame's house.

Augustine seizes my hand and says, "Come on! This is the place to go to today." Her masters are merchants and they tell her where to find the best lard prices, the crispest vegetables, the smoothest butter. I follow her and laugh, I don't know why, but that's how I feel whenever Augustine takes me by the hand. She's tall and scraggy and talks in a loud voice, and she hugs me as if I were a blanket, for she's always cold. While she helps me to fill my food bag with provisions she whispers the town's latest gossip in my ear. Maurice Dupré's slave is getting married to the woman who belongs to old lady Contrefort even though they don't love each other, but their masters believe their offspring will make good workers. Big Lucius Roy was found dead drunk in the arms of Rosalie, Ivain Morelle's servant, the same Rosalie suspected of trying to set her mistress's hair on fire on the night of the feast of Saint-Jean. She was lashed but wasn't tortured like Angélique, the one they hanged in '34 for burning Montreal down.

When I think of Angélique, my stomach goes hollow, as with a sudden hunger. Even though she died before I was born, her story is still on everyone's lips even now. Augustine speaks of her as of a sister; she relates yet again how funny and wicked Angélique was, how she bawled out her mistress, how many times she'd run away before taking her revenge on the white folks of America by torching their city. When I go by the house on Saint-Paul where she once lived, I kneel, pretending to tie my bootlaces. I fear Angélique, I fear her spirit, her big thieving hands; sometimes I'm afraid she might spit on my back because I don't have her courage, her wrath.

Augustine complains her master made a nuisance of himself again last night. She says he's got a wee little prick, yet it never sags and he won't let her sleep. Her master is short and corpulent and everything about him seems to sag, so I can hardly credit what Augustine says about his prick, but one thing's for sure—I'm lucky to have just my mistress. Monsieur died the year I came to their house. His face was as blue as a bad vein and his hands were forever worrying at his watch. Had he been trying to learn the hour of his death, I wonder.

I get back with the provisions, Madame sniffs as she counts the change, and then slips it into her purse. I cook pork and beans, some meat, root vegetables. In the garden, Bertaud sets aside carrots that have grown entwined together like lovers. He brings them to me like treasures. Once, I varnished the roots to try to preserve them, as a bauble, but they turned all black. I threw them away before Bertaud could see. When the weather is fine he brings me the hares he's trapped and, on Friday, the trout he'd caught the night before. But Madame spurns Bertaud's fish because he rips their mouths when he unhooks them. She says the Good Lord is displeased to see his creatures needlessly tormented. I never met anyone more peculiar than Madame.

After supper I clean up the kitchen. I scour the pots and dishes. Each night there's a different chore for me: silver polishing, a counterpane to be woven, socks that need darning, candle-making. When I'm done I knead the bread, fetch a batch of firewood, and stuff the woodstove with logs till it's like a big beating heart. The wall of my bedroom adjoins the stove and I've pushed my bed up close to it. When I lie down for the night I press my hand against the wall. The warmth flows through my skin and I droop like a piece of wool. It's the time of day I like best. When I know that rest is coming. Asleep, I'm no longer Victoria. I'm the girl my mother baptized, I have that name, which is mine alone, and I tumble it around in my mouth and go to sleep.

Madame is holding a grand celebration for her son's return. I've never met him. He's been away five years studying in Paris, beyond the sea and the monsters that dwell in it. He's a lawyer now, and Madame is so very proud. There will be maple syrup cakes, plum wine, cider that tingles inside your head, goose pot pies, and spit-roasted veal in the garden. Bertaud wept when they told him to impale the animal. He hunts hare and trout, but he's too fond of cows to kill their young. That's why Madame asked Cornelius, the neighbour's slave, to take care of it. As for me, I've got more work than I can handle. Luckily the Limoges have agreed to lend us Augustine; the chores turn into merriment. I knead the dough and laugh, Augustine stirs the sauce and laughs, we buff the china and laugh.

The night before the banquet, Augustine is late and in a sullen mood. When I ask her what the matter is she shuts her eyes and moves her head into the steam of the cauldron where the preserves are being made. Her face seems to grow rounder amid the aroma of the fruits. She mutters, "I'm with child." It's the master's. I shudder. I've heard Madame explain to her sister that mulatto women spawn deformed creatures, half-human half-animal, that go up in smoke the instant the curé touches them. As though reading my thoughts, Augustine chides me: "Now don't go alarming yourself with the tales people tell about the bastards of mulattos. That's rubbish, just like all the rest."

Then I feel the joy rising in my gut like a bird escaping from a chimney. I grab Augustine by the hands and start dancing for my friend who's going to give birth to a white man's child. An emancipated baby who one day will set his mother free. Augustine is annoyed and clips me on the head.

"You little fool. When a baby's born to a slave and a master, it inherits the mother's rank. Didn't you know that? My child will never belong to me, he'll be the Limoges' slave. Like you—you were never your mother's daughter."

My nails dig into the skin of my hands.

"That's not so. My mother named me. I'm her daughter."

Augustine clucks her tongue as a sign the conversation is over. We say no more until the noontime meal, when Bertaud chokes on a bean and I manage to expel it by thumping him on the back, which makes Augustine laugh until the tears brim in her eyes.

The next day, Madame goes does down to the harbour while I finish the decorations. We've hung garlands of ivy and placed floral bouquets in every room. It looks for all the world as though the wildest corners of the island have entered the house. At two o'clock I'm at my post. Three girls have come to serve at the table; they speak Portuguese among themselves and I'm sure they're poking fun at me. The guests arrive, you can hear the rustle of taffeta, there are billows of pipe tobacco drifting around, someone makes a speech of which I grasp not a word, then the meal begins, and I fall into a kind of trance. It doesn't stop until there's silence and the three girls bring back the carts full of dirty dishes. My feet throb, my hands tremble, and there's at least five hours of work ahead to get the house shipshape again. Bertaud fell asleep holding a pumpkin in his arms, and I don't have the heart to rouse him.

I'm half-sunk in a basin full of water when I hear someone clearing his throat behind me. A young man with impossible eyes is standing in the doorway. I straighten up.

"I beg your pardon, Miss," he says with a continental accent. "My mother has gone to bed. I've come to suggest you do the same."

I'm struck dumb, so I point to the mess in the dining room.

"It's past two in the morning. You can finish the other rooms tomorrow."

I make a ridiculous curtsy; he stays stock-still before me. I notice his fingers, long and slender and stained with blue ink.

"May I also be so bold as to thank you? The evening was a great success. Your goose pie is simply divine."

He bows and withdraws. His heels make no noise on the floor, as if he weren't really there. When he's disappeared in the stairway, my cheeks flush. Never has anyone called me Miss.

Over the following days, I keep an eye on Hector. I don't dare address him yet, and should I do so it would be as "Monsieur," but in my heart it's Hector, the name I use to conjure him up at night on the warm wall of my little room, the word I caress with my fingertips, the one I gulp down when I'm caught daydreaming. He devotes his days to reading, writing letters, and looking out the window. His mother entreats him to go out, to reacquaint himself with Montreal, but he declines. He says he wishes to make up for the many years far from Madame, though he spends precious little time in her company. In truth, he is afraid. He neither knows nor understands this city and wonders whether he could one day again feel at home here. How I know all this I cannot tell, but I need only look at him to guess his thoughts.

At the market, Augustine has got her nerve back again. She scolds the merchants who sell their flour too dear and points out to me an old, blond-haired Negro woman able, it's said, to cast the evil eye.

"It appears she's the one who visited the whooping cough upon the Gauthier twins, merely because their wet nurse had looked at her askance."

Then she fixes her gaze on me, eyebrows aquiver.

"What ails you today? Did you eat a sick chicken?"

We come across a line of wagons loaded down with grey stones, and it's as if the ground is about to open up and the huge rocks will crush our bones into dust. They're headed to the city's west end, to build the mansions of the English.

"Nothing. Just tired."

The atmosphere in the house has taken on a new texture. Everything is light and objects levitate the moment I go by; there are will-o'-the-wisps hiding behind the furniture. My every gesture becomes a small prayer. I lose the keys three times a day, I eat a chunk of bread and bite the inside of my cheek. Just before the haymaking season it starts pouring rain and the pots in the larder get spattered because of a leak. But instead of wiping away the reddish water, I peel off long petals of wallpaper that have come loose.

Really, truly, madly.

The raspberry bushes are cloaked in red now. Monsieur had an entire hedge of them planted at the far end of the garden. But unlike him, Madame hates raspberries—bad for one's teeth, she says—so we make preserves which I sell in the market in August. I'm entitled to a tenth of the profits. The money buys me new clothes and a few small presents for Augustine. Bertaud has a light touch and he picks the raspberries without making them bleed, but he nicks his fingers. At day's end, I rub them with ointment before he goes home to his elderly mother. His hands are thick and soft as milk.

One morning, Hector comes to join us with a basket under his arm. He makes no noise, but as soon as he steps toward us I sense his presence simply from the way the skin on my back goes taut.

"It looks as though they've all come out at the same time this year! Can I lend a hand?"

I accept his offer, striving not to get lost in his gaze. Standing before a man who has one eye blue and the other green, it's easy to plunge into a hesitation that will hold you in its grip till the end of the world. Hector begins to collect the berries. By the time I've filled my fourth basket, his is barely three-quarters full.

"My, my, aren't you the swift one!"

I look for something courteous and humble by way of a reply, but all that comes out is:

"That's because I don't eat them along the way!"

I want to swallow my tongue and ram my ten fingers down my throat to make sure it won't rise back up. Hector lets out a slight whistle. Lifting my eyes, I realize this is his way of laughing. A fluty, choppy breath. The loveliest laughter I'd ever heard. He slowly extends his bluish hand, holding out a raspberry that lights up the world. I'm at a loss as to what to do. He lowers his hand to mine, which is stupidly fidgeting in my skirt. His skin grazes mine, then he slips the little fruit between my icy fingers. Right then, something gives way inside me, drops down in my belly, and starts to seethe. I toss the berry in my mouth, the bells toll the Angelus. The taste of raspberry floods my body.

Soon after, Hector begins to go out. He takes long walks along the riverside, visits old friends. During his absence, every swing of the clock's pendulum is torture; I'd like to scream for him to come back straightaway. Yet as soon as he arrives I flee to kitchen, almost throwing up, and then it subsides. At night, sleep eludes me, it's too hot and I push my bed far away from the wall, but there's nothing for it, I feel as if I'm inside the stove, swallowed up by its red stomach. My skin seethes beneath the cotton, it tickles, and it hurts so very much. Sometimes, to find some relief, I touch myself and imagine Hector's blue hand swooping down on my body. The pleasure hits home, and I weep and pray the Blessed Virgin for pardon.

Every evening he comes to thank me for my work and to wish me goodnight. Mornings, he comes to say what a glorious day is in the offing. He lingers in the doorway as though waiting for me to speak, but I say nothing and his eyes breathe in mine. One day, he sits down at the little sewing table.

"Tell me, Victoria, if you were not a slave, where would you be?"

"In the Negro graveyard, I suppose."

He gives me a baffled look.

"No, I mean if you were free. What would you like to do?"

Immediately, I think of my mother, of the place where she was laid to rest and where I've never put any flowers. Then I think of that freed panis who became a farmer, and those other slaves who put out to sea.

"I don't know."

Hector nods his head solemnly and goes out. I consider the scissors lying in front of me and have a notion to fling them into the middle of his back.

"What? He asked you that?" Augustine exclaims.

Her belly has begun to show, and she's as pretty as an apple.

"Do you think he wishes to enfranchise me?"

"I shouldn't entertain any illusions if I were you. He's a reader, your master. People who read have strange ideas, but they don't actually do very much."

I shrug and Augustine clucks her tongue. The old blond sorceress waves her over. Augustine excuses herself. "I've got business with Madam Kaliou."

"Madam Kaliou?"

She leans closer.

"She's going to help me take care of my little problem," she mutters, pointing to her belly.

Then she skips away, and I too get the urge to jump until the ground gives way under me feet, until the earth swallows me up.

One morning, I find a slip of paper on the laundry kettle. On it, there are lines of script as delicate as lace, blue as the night. I grasp the paper, trembling, and hold it tight against my body. The sun hasn't yet risen and the world outside is purple. Something on this page whispers my name. Then I hear Bertaud coming and I fold the sheet of paper and hide it in my underpants, against my sex.

In the evening, Hector comes into the kitchen at the usual hour. But rather than wishing me goodnight, he stands there and casts his odd-eyed gaze on me.

"You don't know how to read, do you?" he says at last.

He steps toward me, slowly, and brings his mouth close to my ear. When he begins to speak, an opaque veil shrouds my head and the things around me disappear. He is so close, I hear the air going in and out of him, freighted with his humours.

"I breathe where you quiver / You know; what good is it, alas! / To stay if you leave me / To live if you go away / What good is it to live as the shadow / Of the angel who takes flight? / What good 'neath the darkened sky / To be naught anymore but the night?"

I put my hand over my mouth. I am beautiful, suddenly I'm convinced of this, though I'd never given it any thought until a moment ago. Hector disappears and a deep, exquisite desire to sleep overtakes me. I sink into my bed. I am naught anymore but the night.

The wind blows into the city and the service door rattles all day long as though a succubus were thrashing it to come in. So it takes me a little while to react when someone actually comes knocking. Madame has gone to Quebec City for a few days, Bertaud is in the attic catching mice. I open to find Fifine, the Limoges' young servant, in tears.

"It's Augustine," she sobs.

Augustine, without batting an eye, has swallowed the sorceress Kaliou's potion to get rid of her baby.

"At noon, out came the little dead thing, all grey. Then she began to shiver, she turned pale and now the vicar has come to give her the Last Rites. Maïté says the old woman poisoned her."

My heart stops beating. Behind me I hear Hector's voice. "Go, Victoria." I thank him without turning around and hurry after Fifine.

She is covered in sweat, my beautiful Augustine, and so feverish that the holy oils swim on her forehead. But she recognizes me.

"Victoria. You'll save me."

As if Augustine were deaf, the vicar declares there's nothing to be done. I ask him to sit down and then I turn toward the sufferer. At my former masters' house, the cook was also a midwife and would take me along for the births. I was nine when I delivered my first child and I've not forgotten a thing. I bend down between Augustine's legs and touch her abdomen. She gives me a desperate stare, and this humility, which I'd never seen in her, frightens me far more than her pallor and her shivering. I place my hand on her forehead.

"No half-measures for you, my friend, eh? There's another baby in there. We'll have to get him out."

She groans and the vicar bolts from the room. It's the dead of night when Augustine at last expels the second twin, a small thing, gummy and inert, which the clergyman hastens to bless and carry away. Fifine assists me as I make certain Augustine's belly is quite empty. Her fever has dropped and she's no longer shivering.

"The old woman hasn't poisoned you after all," I say.

Fifine crosses herself as Augustine smiles wanly.

"No, but she well-nigh killed me all the same."

We embrace through our sticky shawls, and I leave the Limoges' house at dawn. Place Royale is deserted, save for a sleeping drunkard propped against a horse more dignified than him. When I get home, Hector comes down in his nightshirt.

"How is your friend?"

"She is safe and sound."

My skirts ripple around my ankles as if they were alive. I find myself, I don't know how, standing a few inches from Hector. Outside, the wind lays into the leaves and sets the trees swaying. I gather his face in both my hands and bring it close to mine. His mouth is a chapel and my entire soul kneels within it. I'm blind and my ears are whistling. When we move apart and Hector leaves, the kitchen empties altogether, nothing remains. I slip into my room. Near my bed, the stove wall glows as red as hot coals.

Madame, back from Quebec City, exclaims, "Our Victoria, a midwife! Who would have thought! The Limoges are in our debt—just imagine if they had had to buy a new slave!"

Her cousins in Quebec City told her that smoking is a cure for headaches. Now rose-coloured wreaths trail after her throughout the house, and she coughs in her sleep. She goes to bed early, and no sooner has she retired than Hector comes to me. The time we spend together escapes through a hole in time. He unbraids my hair, I slide my fingers between his shirt buttons, and in these few gestures three hours are swallowed up. He makes as if to take his leave, and I can't bring myself to let him go. Mornings find me enervated, the survivor of a luminous battle.

He is as smooth as the surface of water, as the first day of a life. His scent is that of mint and great journeys. His caresses bring to mind the age before death, and I sing him songs I'd long forgotten. He wants to undress me, to possess me completely, but I'm too afraid of what very nearly killed Augustine, I beseech him to stop and he stops. We breathe very hard, it hurts between my legs and then he goes and kisses that burning place, assuring me that this is not how children are made, and I dare not reply that what awaits us instead is hell.

He believes the streets are dangerous. Last week, a band of soldiers dragged a slave woman by the hair and dishonoured her till she lost the power of speech. This took place at night, in one of the poorer quarters, but I go out only in the daytime. Still, Hector says he fears for me, and he follows me from a distance, hidden among the crowd. He wants to stay close to me. It makes me smile. As I've fallen behind in my chores on account of our evenings, he lends me a hand. He pricks his fingers with my needles, the candles he makes are all crooked, and I nearly wake Madame with my guffaws. He kisses my fingernails and my eyelids, and I press my hand against his heart. There are times I doubt he truly exists.

Somehow Augustine realizes what's going on. She chides me.

"Silly girl. You think he's going to take you out of your kitchen? He's going to ruin your life—that's what'll happen. It amuses them to make us believe in love."

She's unaware of the pain her words cause me, otherwise she would keep quiet.

"It's not unheard of, a white man marrying a Negro woman. The Smiths, the people who came from the Great Lakes, they're married," I tell her.

"They're poor. Rich folk aren't like that. They never wed slaves."

I feel a lump in my throat. She's right and I hate her. I scurry home in tears, and I can hear Hector running behind me. Madame is playing cards with her friends and doesn't notice when I come in. Hector must stay to chat with them. His voice is different when he speaks to his mother's friends and this vexes me. I have no way of knowing whether he dissembles with them or with me. He finally arrives after supper and steps toward me. Immediately I start to weep again.

"I don't want you coming to see me anymore."

He stops short, as if I'd dealt him a blow to the stomach.

"Why?"

"Because you're just amusing yourself with me. You'll cast me off when you're done."

His eyes grow wide and for the first time the green and the blue seem to blend. "That's not true."

"Masters never wed their slaves, everyone knows that."

"That may be so here. But elsewhere it's different. The world is changing, Victoria. Soon there will be no more slaves."

"Is that what you believe?"

"It's what I wish."

"So why haven't you enfranchised me yet? What are you waiting for?"

"I'm waiting for my mother to convey to me the deeds of property that my father bequeathed to her."

I don't know what to answer. Behind me, the eggs are bouncing around in the boiling water, they're overcooked now and a sulphury stench wafts up from the pot. Hector approaches and embraces me.

"I love you, Victoria."

At nightfall he refuses to leave and persuades me to let him lie down in my little bed. I can't stop the tears, he enfolds me in his arms. Just before dozing off I'm gripped by a wild urge to tell him my name, burning on the edge of my lips, turning hard as a bullet. But then I'm submerged in dreams.

Tears are the verbena of the heart, they bring on sleep. Nestled one against the other, we're unaware of the dawn. It's Madame who wakes us. My first impression is that she has doused us with a bucketful of cold water, but, no, the sheets are dry to my touch. Hector leaps up and follows his mother, who stomps across the house in a rage. As I rub my swollen eyes, I hear her shouting through the door of the library.

"How many times have I warned you! These Negresses are all strumpets!"

I discern Hector's voice trying to calm her, but I'm unable to make out his words. Nor can Madame hear them, apparently. From the thumping noises, I gather she is hurling books.

"First it was your father with that wench of a Greta, and now you! You're sick! Well, I know a proper remedy for that!"

My cheeks flame up. Monsieur and Greta. I should have understood long ago. Thoughts race through my mind. If Greta was sold for frolicking with Monsieur, will I come to the same end? I spin in circles while redoing my braids.

Bertaud, who has a great knack for sensing an approaching storm, has taken shelter in the garden, amid the frost, where he makes a show of picking fruits that will never ripen. I busy myself in the kitchen trying to reassure myself. Hector will smooth things over. If he doesn't manage to reason with his mother he'll surely find a way of buying me from her. The bread in the oven refuses to rise.

Madame and Hector stay shut inside the library for nearly an hour. When I hear doors slamming I let the potatoes rest and press my back against a beam, as if standing to attention. Madame enters the kitchen.

"Victoria, your presence in this house has become intolerable. My cousins in Chambly, the Tousignants, are in need of someone. You'll go there tomorrow."

Inside me, a sack full of sand falls without landing anywhere, as if down a gaping well. The Tousignants have dozens of slaves working the fields. They're driven like animals. The slow ones are beaten.

"Where is Hector?" I stammer.

Madame's face grows taut, her lips entirely disappear, and she gives me a slap that makes everything go blue for a second.

"That's one question you won't be asking ever again. Understood?"

All the livelong day I do nothing else but weep. Bertaud brings me little flowers that he's picked on the fringe of the garden, in the tangled corners that I couldn't tame. I'd like to go there now, to burrow into the rotten leaves and let the horseflies devour me. Bertaud taps me on the shoulder. I ought to bid him farewell but can't bring myself to do it; I can't believe this is how it will end. Hector doesn't come back, and I pray he'll find a notary or a priest kind enough to help him get me out of here.

At the headache hour, Augustine comes scratching on the service door.

"They told me what's happened. How dreadful, Victoria."

"It's not over. Hector's going to straighten things out. He wants to enfranchise me. He told me so yesterday."

Closing her eyes with an air of hopelessness, Augustine proffers a little basket.

"Hush up, and take this. There's still time to save your skin. You're so young. Forget your Monsieur and do what you must do. I love you, my friend."

She kisses me and dashes away. Her big, dry arms break up in the autumn mist. The front door slams, and I slide the basket under my bed. I cock my ear and my shoulders sag even more. It's not Hector but a friend of Madame. They smoke and fill the house with poison.

When evening comes I'm incapable of holding still. Hector has not yet returned, and Bertaud won't leave, like a cat that knows rain is on the way. I kneel down before my medal of St. Mark and pray very hard for forgiveness, for my wish to be fulfilled, for love, for salvation. Around ten o'clock, something is slipped under the door. I grasp the paper and quickly lift the flap. A young boy, a stranger to me, moves off at a casual pace. I unfold the paper and Hector's blue script scrolls out, powerless to provide me with the slightest explanation. My sobs redouble, out of anger and love, while I hold the message with my fingertips, as if it were about to take wing and carry off my last chance to be rescued. Nearby, Bertaud is breathing like an ox. He gently takes the letter from me and his voice, deep as a church organ, rises in the room.

"'What shall I, withdrawn, alone, / make of the day and the sky without you, / Of my kisses without your mouth, / Of my tears without your eyes!'"

He pauses, stares at me, then slowly adds:

"And below it says, 'Forgive me, Victoria.'"

So astonished am I to hear Bertaud reading out these words that I need a little while to grasp their meaning. Hector won't be coming. I'm lost. I turn toward this man, so large and so gentle that he has saved his voice for this one moment. I stroke his cheek.

"Thanks, Bertaud. You go home now."

The look he gives me is heart-rending, but he obeys. Once he's gone into the night, I feel as though I've finished something. I put away the remaining pieces of cutlery in the kitchen, and I collect my medals. I examine the basket that Augustine brought me. In it, there's a loaf of bread, half a ham, three cheeses, a knife, a tinder light, a woollen bonnet, and a handful of pieces of sugar. She'll no doubt be punished for stealing it all from her masters. I hug the bonnet against my breast and slip a cube of sugar between my lips. The taste fills my mouth and shakes my limbs. When I go out, a biting wind stings my face.

The night is very dark, but the clouds moored to Mount Royal send forth a glow that guides me. I skim across the avenues chilled by the approach of All Saints' Day and by the lurking dead. Tonight, they've agreed to take under their wings a poor fool who believed that love would free her. Sheltered by the shadows, I trot, I run, I stride over the puddles, I go along the rows of naked trees and the monastery walls.

The mountain draws closer. I offer up my flight to it, I hold out my hand to it. I'm an arrow, and my whole being aspires to the north, where slaves are protected by impassable swamps, by tree trunks as broad as bell towers, and moose bearing sovereign antlers. I remember, I saw them, just before my mother died in our cabin, killed by liberty, it seemed. A few weeks later I returned to the farm whence we'd fled, too young to make it on my own in the vast choir of the northern forests. But now I'm big, I'm strong. I'll be able to chop wood, to keep the fire going, to slit throats and don the skins of the beasts I kill. I'll be a queen, the queen of the spirits that the Indians let loose upon those who know how to take but not create, to do but not dream.

Only when I reach the first ramparts of rock do I hear them. The echoes carry the sound of their steps, the shouts of their throats. They've brought dogs, I catch a whiff of their musky odour. It's for me they've come. Madame must have foreseen my escape—why hadn't I thought of it? She hired the men this morning to watch me, unless they're in the colony's service, charged with tracking runaway slaves. I start to run.

The mountain is steep. I scramble up the slope. After a few minutes I'm short of breath and the basket feels heavy. Below I can see the grey stone districts, with the horses of the English, who sleep under heavy blankets like princes. I'm hot in my woollens, and my feet, too small for my boots, rub against the rough leather. I keep climbing.

The forest is truly a labyrinth. I twist and turn in the darkness not knowing if it's up or down, if I've come closer to the summit or to the men hunting for me. Suddenly, I arrive at a promontory. I nearly plunge but I seize a branch and hold on. Montreal is spread out before me, its torches striving to illuminate the dense waters of the night. Somewhere beneath one of those flames Hector is awake. He is surely aware of my flight by now. I picture him tremulously reading once again his books of poetry—they're no use to us now—his forehead beaded with sweat, the blue of his hands engulfing the world. In a flash, my thoughts spring up from where I'd buried them. I hurt in a place I'd never known of, the place in my body that hates the man I continue to love so fervently, and that hates me for letting myself be ruined by one so craven. I am exposed. The barking comes nearer.

When the first shot rings out it appears to come from all sides at once, as though the city and the mountain were assailing me in unison. My first thought was of that famous barrel of powder that served to buy me seven years ago. I wonder if it's the same gunpowder, if I'm being slain by the thing that already slew me a hundred times. I look for a tree, a rock to shield me, but my legs won't budge, they're full of Hector. I think of Augustine, of her mouth tucked into a grain sack pillow, repeating the words, "silly girl, silly girl," for hours on end. The shots multiply, I try to mumble a prayer, to touch my medals, but even this is beyond me, and it occurs to me that I may already be dead.

A stifling heat explodes in the middle of my chest. My fingers reach for the spot, searching in the sticky fluid that seeps through my clothes for a strand, a thread I can grasp. The smell of blood envelops me, the dogs bark louder. I'm still on my feet, my legs hold me up, and the night lights up imperceptibly. Then I hear nothing. Nothing but a sort of rustling about my head, as if time were unfurling on either side of my face to lead me back to its beginnings. I clasp my hands tightly together, very tightly. For an hour, two perhaps, I was free. A great bonfire flares up in my back.

SHE KNOWS she's seen him before somewhere. The feeling shouldn't come as a surprise, here, at the local studios of the national TV network. But nothing about him suggests an actor or a news anchorman. He looks like a man accustomed not to being watched but to watching others, and each of his gestures evinces kindness.

Then she notices the object that he's set down by his feet, next to a plastic bag.

"Is that Queen Victoria?" she asks, pointing to the picture.

He looks up.

"Yes, it's for my daughter."

He lifts up the little portrait, examines it, and then turns it toward the woman, as if to invite her and the sovereign to exchange hellos.

"You don't miss a thing," he adds with a smile.

"Let's just say that Victorias tend to catch my eye."

"The same goes for me. Are you here for the interview?"

Almost disappointedly, the woman nods yes. For months now she's garnered many such coincidences, traces of Victoria in her daily life. She would have liked for this one to be purely a matter of luck.

"And what is your connection with Madame Victoria?" she inquires.

"I'm the one who found her. Her body. Her skull, to be exact."

"Oh, you're Germain Léon!"

He arches his eyebrows in surprise. The woman holds out her hand.

"Céleste Hippolyte. I worked on the case, that's how I know your name. You're something of a legend to us."

"No!" Germain protests.

"Oh, yes! You were the starting point! She chose to make herself known through you."

Germain chuckles. She's a strange one, this detective. He decides he likes her.

"So, still no leads?"

Céleste shakes her head. Afraid she might take his question as criticism, Germain studies her face, gives her a benevolent little smile, and looks down again at the portrait of the queen resting in his hands.

"It isn't easy to get out of our Victorian era, is it?" he continues.

Céleste's face suddenly opens up in agreement.

"I think she'll be with me for the rest of my life," she adds.

They haven't noticed Loïc's arrival. But Loïc heard Céleste's comment, and something inside him shuddered. He'd like to respond. He'd like to tell them—this bright woman and this gentle-eyed nurse—about his quest. But time is short and the camera crew is waiting.

"Ms. Hippolyte, Mr. Léon, I'm Loïc. We spoke on the phone. You're on next."

Germain and Céleste follow the reporter through the maze of the building. Loïc introduces them to the program host and then returns to his office. The interviews that eventually come out of his preparatory conversations are always a letdown. The material provided by these two, in whose minds Madame Victoria has lodged just as she has in his, will amount to just a thin substratum.

On his table lies a gleaming collection of photos, with the halogen glare bouncing off their glossy finish. The portraits stare back at him. Women with auburn hair, blonds, a few redheads, Slavs, Hispanics, blacks, and an appalling number of Indigenous women. They all seem to belong to the same family, united by an elusive commonality: they're unaware of what awaits them, they're carefree yet somehow haunted. Unless it's just Loïc projecting this feeling onto the pictures. Most of these missing women probably had good reason to be sad, but also a thousand reasons to unbridle their joy, their hope, their delight at being young and having a whole life of experiences, errors, and exploits still ahead of them.

Edgar, Loïc's supervisor, pops in unannounced, walks over to Loïc's desk, and glances at the series of photos fanned out on it.

"They've started the shoot with Léon?"

"Yes, and with Céleste Hippolyte," Loïc answers.

"Excellent. What about you? Still leaving for Victoria tomorrow?"

"Vancouver, not Victoria."

"Right. That's what I meant."

The two men quickly go over Loïc's next report, an assignment that will let him move on without moving on. Instead of an unidentified corpse, he'll be investigating women whose names are known but whose bodies have never been found, a negative of the Victoria case. She may not have died a violent death, but the fact remains there's something violent about her solitude, an oblique kind of cruelty that Loïc is trying to delineate.

While Loïc gathers his papers, Edgar goes back to scanning the pictures.

"What exactly is the point of collecting all these headshots?"

Loïc shrugs. For days now, he's been evasive, hoping he can avoid explaining to his manager that his investigation is turning into a sort of art project, his analyses into meditations. That he's looking for meaning in these faces captured on paper rather than in the police reports. That he's yet another boy from a maimed family looking for answers in the wrong places.

He's just about to stammer out some lame justification when he's saved by the telephone. As soon as he catches sight of the regional code on the display he claps his hand over the receiver and signals to Edgar that he has to take the call.

The serial killer's ex-wife speaks with a tired voice, as if she's been dragging a dead body for a long time. No introductions, no explanation. Like an old acquaintance, she says:

"It's Deborah. You wanted to talk to me about Rob?"

Loïc immerses himself again in the case of the trucker locked away for multiple murders of young female hitchhikers, one of the worst serial killings in the history of the United States. He tries to imagine the person at the other end. This woman, breathing slowly, had she known what kind of man she'd married? The first time she heard the charges brought against him, did she believe them? Was she a victim of his violent personality? The questions Loïc would like to ask vie with those he must ask. But before he can come out with the first one, Deborah stops him.

"Listen," she says, "there's just one thing I'm going to tell you about my ex. About what he did. Just a little story, actually. Do what you want with it."

Loïc reaches for his notepad, rummages for a pen in the clutter of his desk. Deborah has already gone ahead.

"When we were still married—before Rob got arrested—I sometimes rode along with him on his runs. One time we were at a highway truck stop. A teenager walked past us, you know, a ragged girl in army boots, lugging a huge backpack. Rob watched her walk away. After a bit he says to me: 'Y'see that? That girl—she's one of the invisible people.' That's what Rob had to say about those women he hunted down. That's what I had to say about Rob."

With that, Deborah hangs up. Loïc realizes he's been holding his breath since the conversation began. "The invisible people," he mutters. He turns to his gallery of photos, examines them closely and recalls those names: Robert Ben Rhoades, William Fyfe, Paul Bernardo, Ted Bundy, Robert Pickton. Then he sits down, grabs a sheet of paper, a pencil. What he wants to do can't be done on a computer. It takes the rasp of a pen on a page, the scraping, the abrasion. It means feeling, eyes closed, the letters being etched into the paper. While Germain Léon and Céleste Hippolyte, each in their own way, describe the black hole that has run through their lives, while his colleagues tap away at their keyboards and drone into their mics, while one more woman vanishes and the long Road of Tears grows longer, Loïc writes down the first name on the list.

There are thousands.

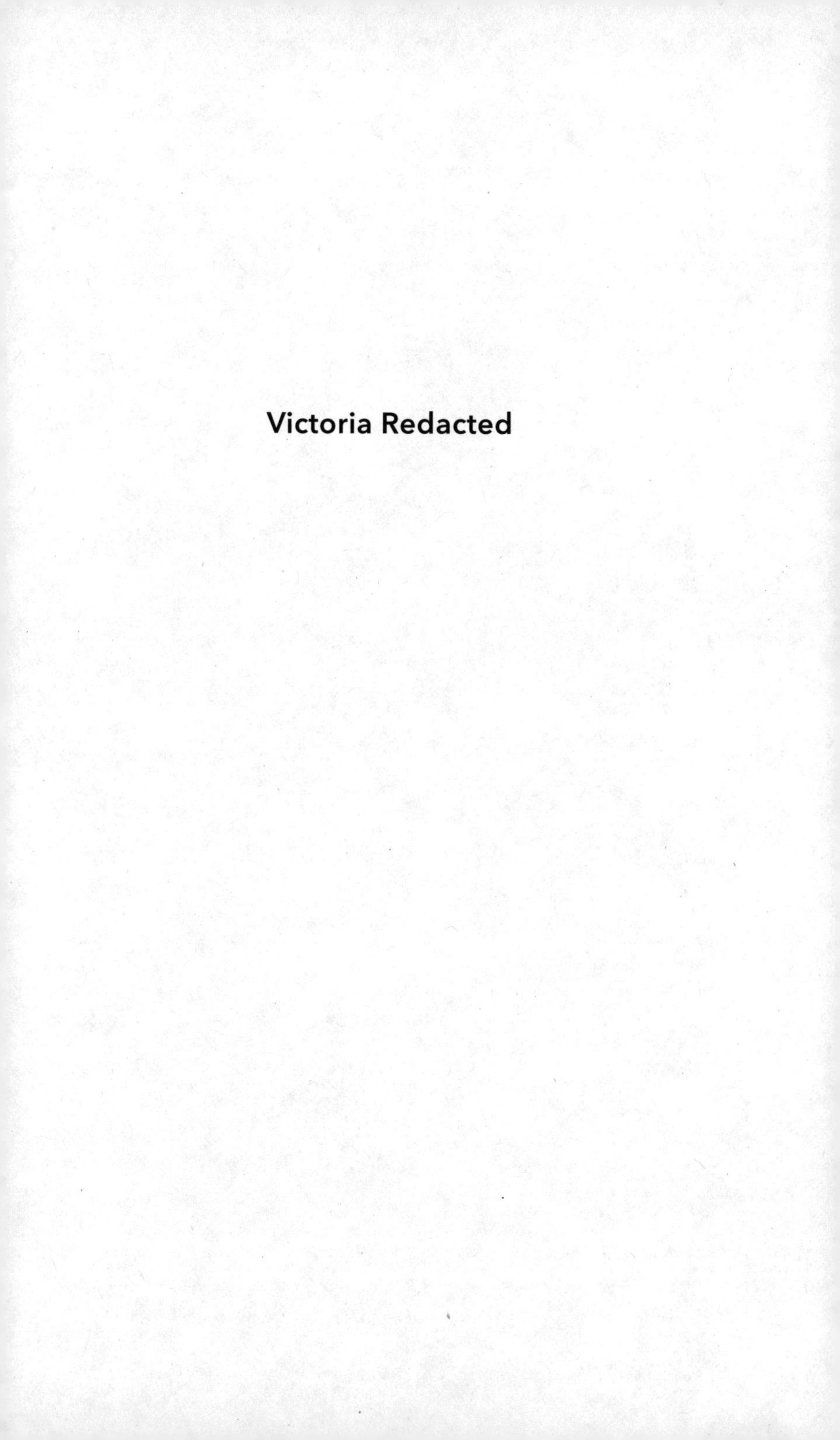

Victoria Redacted

RAGE WAS SOMETHING Victoria had never felt until she became invisible.

Yes, she had lost control at times and had vented her anger. Like everyone else, she had hated her share of foes and former lovers. But ever since her metamorphosis, her fury has reached heights that she hadn't thought possible. In fact, many things she hadn't thought possible have come true. Her transparency, for one. Her existence in this hospital's absurd ecology, for another.

For months, she has ranged over the Royal Victoria's twisted passageways, its diagonal elevators, its secret mezzanines leading from the eighth floor of one building to the ground floor of a different wing. She has explored the balconies precariously perched on roofs skewed by the wind, climbed staircases that catapulted her from Monday to the previous Sunday. She has found herself suddenly outside, stuck between a stone wall and the slope of the mountain or plunged in a ditch littered with old bandages and crumbs of life. She spent three days locked inside a closet banging on a pipe until someone from maintenance opened the door. At the Royal Victoria it's easy to be forgotten. To disappear.

Occasionally, she follows the people ambling down the corridors adorned with Gothic moulding; they act as a kind of Ariadne's thread guiding her through the labyrinth. She silently breathes in the conversations of the regulars, their whispers full of innuendos. The story she hears most often is the ghost legend. The ghost of the nurse murdered in the west block. The ghost of the mad chef who cooked elderly patients. The ghost of the gardener who had his throat ripped open by a wolf a hundred years ago. The ghost of the young mother who died giving birth to quintuplets. The ghost of the schizophrenic who drowned in the hospital swimming pool. The ghost of every neglected, malnourished, unloved patient who came back to settle accounts. Rubbish—all of it! There's only one ghost in this hospital, and it's Victoria.

Every morning, in the nook where she's taken up residence, her hatred awakens when she does. Victoria wends her way among the convalescents, snatches a spongy egg or two in the cafeteria right under the cashier's nose, and starts her daily quest, reciting an inaudible refrain that reminds her of everything she has lost. A reasonably functional family. Muscular legs. An underpaid job. A proud demeanour. Eccentric friends. A charming smile. A passion for hip-hop and origami. An unruly head of hair. A university degree. Freckles. Five credit cards. A healthy BMI. A predilection for dance floors. A shadow that lengthened through the day and faded at nightfall.

The advertisement had said: *Our tests meet the highest safety standards. Participants will not undergo any process that has not been certified risk-free.* Victoria was reassured. And there was more: *Volunteers receive from $1,000 to $2,250 in financial compensation. Open to non-smokers only.* That was all she needed to know. Two thousand two hundred and fifty dollars would cover a year's tuition for the master's degree she was hoping to pursue. It represented half of her outstanding credit card balance. It meant eating meat and vegetables until the end of the winter.

She went to the laboratory tucked away in a basement in the McGill Ghetto district hard by the Royal Victoria. She shook the left hands of the other participants—their right hands had been punctured by syringes—and munched on the cookies handed out to the volunteers while a company representative explained the tests they were about to undergo. She wondered why there was no company sign on the door and why the place had no windows. She tried not to think about the eventual side effects, and repeated to herself the promised sum of money.

She knows now that not all laboratory rats are confined to cages. Some are found in the hospital that has become her home. She learned that they are not all compensated and some of them had not even given their consent. That their illness goes deeper than the worst kind of cancer because it was produced by practitioners who don't respect the Hippocratic oath any more than thieves respect the Eighth Commandment. When she looks at them she feels pain in her arms, her cheeks, every spot where she had received unproven drugs or incomplete treatments. At night she strokes their damp foreheads, sometimes resisting the urge to shake these people who thoughtlessly swallow whatever they're offered, never questioning, and to thrash the nurses, perfectly oblivious to what's going on. It's a lesson she learned at great cost: one person is cured at the expense of hundreds of others.

Yet for all the horrors she has witnessed at the Royal Victoria, she has also discovered inexhaustible kindness running through the actions of the weary staff. She can taste the calmness emanating from the patients waiting for remission or death or the good-heartedness of their fellows. She watches alongside them as the IV slowly drips from a transparent bag like a jellyfish. The time of the illness calculated in drops of solution. The acquiescence of those for whom the system is always too slow. This hospital has a knack for deflating the vindictive moods of those in its care. Except for Victoria's, of course. Revenge is her sole raison d'être. Without it she would have evaporated altogether.

The first trials went well. She spent a few days in a clinic together with other students, unemployed workers, and a handful of lunatics convinced that they were taking part in a grand scientific odyssey. She submitted to examinations, blood pressure tests, blood samples, an array of questionnaires, and went back home with a greater awareness of her body and the networks underlying her breathing, her digestion, her existence. Dr. Eon, who coordinated the tests, was quite pleased with her participation. He said she had a "very reactive" system and "eloquent" vital signs. Victoria smiled at these strange compliments without paying much attention to this dreary-aged man. As soon as the examinations were over she pocketed her phenomenal cheque and returned home.

When Dr. Eon contacted her about a new research protocol that he was in charge of, she was unsuspicious. This trial required, in his words, a "broader degree of consent" than the previous ones. When Victoria asked if it was dangerous, Eon gave a little cough that was his version of laughter and assured her that no drug designed to treat a condition as benign as acne could harm a woman radiating health like her. He added that the compensation would be twice the usual amount. Victoria thought of the upcoming spring break, of the rich kids at the university who were planning trips to the Caribbean, and agreed.

The time when she was consumed with bitter anger toward herself, toward her recklessness back then, that time had long passed. She was young, she was eager, she had been fooled. As she strides along the hospital corridors, her rage is an arrow pointing due north. It's Eon she wants to destroy, torture, devour so she can spit him out as food for the most loathsome creatures, the ones unable to hunt anymore and that stupidly wait for another animal to throw them a bone, a nail, a useless appendage.

But even with the advantages of invisibility, Victoria hasn't been able to catch the doctor, whose right eye says blue, while his left eye says green. When she does manage to get her hands on a vague schedule, a shifting appointment, she always arrives too late. She loses her way or learns that an emergency has taken Eon somewhere else. She runs through the sprawling buildings only to discover that from one day to the next the dermatology clinic has been moved to the other end of the hospital, which she reaches, out of breath, a minute after the department's constantly changing office hours have ended.

One day, a card appears at her feet, as jarring as an unexpected lump of salt on the tongue: *Dr. Eon, room 303, 12th floor, Pavilion E.* Victoria triumphantly takes off, regretting only that she doesn't have time to lay hands on a knife or the poisoned cocktail that she dreams of administering to the doctor. Doesn't matter, she tells herself as she runs down the windy corridors. Her fury makes all sorts of murders possible; even the most innocuous-looking weapon can deal out a brutal death.

But before she even tries to activate the antiquated machinery of the E block elevator, Victoria realizes the Royal Victoria's peculiarities have thwarted her once again. There is no button for number 12 on the panel because Pavilion E does not have a twelfth floor. In her exasperation, she punches the elevator door so hard that the passengers inside jump in terror and pull the emergency lever. Powerless to overcome the ghosts, the alarm keeps on sounding in the E wing to no effect. It seems to have been ringing forever. Since the day Victoria vanished.

As she sat down in the room where the tests were performed, she found it odd that she was the only participant. Equally bizarre, she thought, was that the person administering the treatment was Dr. Eon himself rather than an assistant, as was usually the case. While he coated Victoria's body with a bluish substance, the silence in the research centre grew heavy and oppressive. The doctor's fingers rubbed every centimetre of skin, digging into the flesh, worming into the slightest folds. Naked and shivering under the greasy glaze, Victoria clenched her teeth and pressed her knees together. After what seemed like an eternity, Eon pulled off his gloves. "And now, stage number two."

The day wore on in an endless series of alchemical manoeuvres to which Victoria submitted, shivering the whole time, unable to get over her anxiety, which was out of character for her. The one thing that kept her from bolting naked down the freezing air-conditioned corridors was the promise of five thousand dollars in hard cash. That night, without saying a word, Eon pointed her to a bed, more like a stretcher, and went away. Although she was alone, Victoria thought she could hear the laboured breathing of another patient, someone heavy and worn out. Terrified, she gnawed at the belly of the night until she found her way to sleep.

The next day she awoke with no idea of the time, certain that Eon had come to observe her while she slept. There was a cold meal on a platter but she wasn't hungry. Her limbs felt limp and hollow, as if every cell of her body had emptied out. She put a hand to her forehead, to her knee, and the too-smooth texture of her skin made her dizzy. "Is anyone there?" she wanted to say. But no sound came out of her mouth, and she couldn't see her fingers when she grasped the doorknob. She looked down at her body. In the place where, yesterday, her chest rose and fell in time with her breathing, there was nothing. In the place where her feet should have trodden the floor, there was the floor and nothing else. In a panic, she hit the fire alarm. Despite the deafening noise, no help appeared, nor did her body. Eon had erased her.

The following months were divided between grieving and struggling to convince her relations of her existence. In their bereavement, they had come to believe in ghosts rather than an unseeable Victoria. Her helplessness drove her into frenzied efforts to persuade them that she was shouting despite her silence, and that her invisibility had not expunged her from the world. But what followed confirmed what she had always somehow intuited: the spirit is nothing, the body is everything. To be unseen is to be nonexistent.

No matter how much she moved the furniture around in her mother's house or banged on things in classrooms or grabbed her friends' pencils to write desperate messages, all she managed to do was terrify the people she wished to comfort. She therefore decided to distance herself from her loved ones, feeling more comfortable in the company of strangers than among those to whom she could no longer convey either distress or affection. Only occasionally did she make an exception and watch the lights in her parents' windows or those of her former lovers, her exhausted eyes shedding dry tears.

Her hopes that the effects of Dr. Eon's treatment would be temporary faded as well. Victoria was definitely and irremediably invisible. True, she could douse herself with paint, or wear clothes, something she had persisted in doing out of habit for some time after the calamity. There again, her efforts did nothing but arouse a keen sense of horror in others as well as herself. Even now, her transparency stifles her. She often thinks of the sci-fi films and comics she devoured as a teenager, where invisibility was an enviable power. But the fact is it's not a gift; it's a curse.

When she lies down in pitch darkness, she touches her arms, her legs, which, though absent, have remained solid and muscular; she cups her breasts and notes how they've changed shape over the years. Sometimes out of desperation as much as need, she steals into the room of a young comatose man who has retained certain reflexes, draws back his sheets, strokes him through his hospital gown, and then silently straddles him behind the warm curtains, trembling and nervous, as if someone could surprise her. Her partner ejaculates, she tumbles down into the gorge of her own orgasm, and for a brief instant she wants for nothing. She leaves the alcove trying to believe it did her victim as much good as it did her. Then she returns to her closet downright disgusted with herself.

Over time, she's grown used to the Royal Victoria, its dusty hallways, the red-faced medical students, the snarling wives demanding answers, and all those sighs, the prodigious first breaths and the painful last gasps of the patients. She envies those who are touched, hugged, gazed at so that their image might never be forgotten. The ones looked at with love or even with contempt—what does it matter? At least they feel the touch of someone's eyes, a kind of caress all the same.

Each day the hospital reveals a new side of itself to her. Sometimes it's a dilapidated gym or a dormitory for tired emergency doctors or a storeroom full of cribs from another era. Then, one morning, the institution that has thrown so many obstacles in her path finally hands her a treasure. A wall in its most austere wing is dominated by a bronze and polished oak board, gleaming brightly, a sun in the clinical caverns. It shows the names of doctors with the words IN and OUT beside each one. A sliding wooden slat is positioned to indicate whether the doctor is present or not. Exultant, Victoria spots Eon's name beside a shining IN. Her thoughts are racing, her invisible canine teeth grow longer. Her mind's eye sees the scalpels on the third floor. The electrodes in the intensive care unit. The wire of a lamp snatched from a lounge. She's got him at last.

Ignoring the people brushing past her, she plants herself in front of the board, trembling from head to foot. This intensity gives her the feeling that she has re-entered the tangible world, that she has rediscovered its shine and shadows. One by one, the doctors file past and gently shift the wooden slats, as if the entire hospital has slowed down while they perform this old-fashioned yet crucial act. In the late afternoon, the traffic grows denser; Victoria twiddles her invisible hair, which hisses like combustible gas. Eon is not among the group leaving the building, but she doesn't despair. The light declines, conversations become muffled, the ventilation system grumbles neurotically.

It's past midnight when she hears sharp footsteps approaching. Victoria shudders. Dark silhouette, bald skull, eyes of different colours—all exactly like the image her memory raises up. The ambient oxygen level drops. Victoria has stopped breathing. Eon gingerly steps up to the board, eyeing it like it was about to blow up in his face. He lifts his arm, lets his hand hover before his name. Then, as if the slat weighed a ton, he laboriously brings the word OUT into view. He glides toward the door followed by Victoria, beside herself with anticipation. As he crosses the threshold of the hospital, Victoria hesitates momentarily. She hasn't left this place for ages. The streets, the noise, the hectic air rattle her. The night is within reach. Eon dives into the darkness. Victoria takes a deep breath and gives chase.

He appears to have heard her running behind him. He stops, peers into the shadows for a moment, then continues on his way. Victoria frantically looks around for a weapon. The innumerable possibilities provided by the hospital recede as she moves farther away from it. After a few hundred metres, the din of Avenue des Pins swells and Victoria pictures herself pushing Eon under the wheels of a truck. But he doesn't head toward the street. Instead, he plunges into the woods like a wolf.

All the hate that sustained Victoria these last years is now concentrated in her body. She swoops down on Eon in a wild rush. Going all out, she locks his throat in the crook of her arm, as though she were not just invisible but improbably endowed with superhuman strength. Eon easily breaks free, and when he throws his attacker her head dashes against the stony ground. She is dazed but stands back up and renews her assault, this time wielding a branch with which she lays into her enemy. As he fends off the blows, Eon searches the motionless night for an explanation. At last he understands. "I knew you'd come back one day," he mutters. He grabs away her club and whirls it around him to keep his adversary at bay.

Victoria goes deeper into the woods, still dizzy with pain from the injury to her head. She suspects she's bleeding; her right temple feels wet. Groping about, she lays hands on a rock, and the cold, implacable touch of granite emboldens her. Straining, she straightens up and lifts the rock. Her muscles have been metallized. The projectile must weigh fifty pounds. Clasping it against her breast, she charges ahead in pursuit of Eon. Once she is within range, she hurls the rock with all her might. In the darkness, she hears the impact and then a groan. The man has been hit in the back. Coming closer, she sees him stretched out full length. She picks up her weapon and in a single predatory motion slams it down on Eon's skull. The crunch pierces the silence. Without uttering even one of the words she dreamed of spitting in his face, Victoria lifts her rock once more and strikes him again and again, until Eon disintegrates.

After staring at the corpse for several minutes, Victoria knows that it's over. Nothing else will happen, Eon won't disappear, there is nothing to be learned from his carcass. There will be no explanation, no revelation. She turns toward the horizon, the downtown skyline. What better way to greet this victory than to see the metropolis glittering like stolen treasure? But all Victoria can feel is the burning sensation eating away at the right side of her head. The ferrous smell is everywhere. She's thirsty. She staggers forward through the sapling branches, her thoughts in a jumble. The churning of air conditioners clamps the wood in a black vise.

She finds herself in a clump of wintergreen, judging from the fragrance that rises from her feet to her head. She breathes in and it occurs to her that she too has a scent that other people actually may have kept on detecting while she believed she was all alone in the world, an olfactory marker she might have used to communicate, like cats, dogs, and all animals familiar with the unseen. Then her thoughts crumble. She curls up into what's left of her and collapses in the fragrant herbs.

The night wears on, her oblivion grows thicker. If, in the morning, someone had stood nearby, they would have noticed amid the first rays of light and the sighs of the city, an opalescent skin, a tired body materializing in disparate bits. Brittle at first, the features would have taken on a smoother texture, revealing the arch of an eyebrow, a protruding collarbone, the outline of a knee, a breath fixed on dry lips. But there is no one. The dawn is empty, empty and cold for undefeated women.

Victoria as Woman

LIKE MANY THINGS in his life, this didn't start with a wish but a duty. His superiors had told him: "It takes a man to finish the job, but it'll take a woman to get the ball rolling." He'd laughed, having always considered himself a man who didn't waver, who wasn't ambiguous like some of his more delicate colleagues; in sum, a male whose maleness couldn't be dissimulated. But most of all he was obedient, so he had agreed to play the game—willingly. It would be fun.

He was to neutralize a traitor. A fat Moscow vulgarian, rotten to the tips of his sausage-like fingers, who cheerfully jumped from one camp to the other, clearly for the Americans' benefit. The agents who went about transforming Maslo had carefully researched the target's preferences: brown hair, dark complexion, large bosom. Maslo had to acquire the ABCs of cosmetics. First, the skin. Given his distant Khorasani roots, the bronze hue of his complexion was in no need of enhancement, but it was necessary to mask some very telling scars.

Next, the eyes, which he was taught to enlarge and darken to give them a feline appearance that was then softened by eyebrows shaped to a pointed arch so as to produce an air of surprise. Astonishment, he learned, was the formidable weapon of the femme fatale. On the big night, he'll need to put the final touches on this look with false eyelashes fastened with a nasty, vinegar-smelling glue, the only kind resistant to the sweat that invariably breaks out over a truly male body all the way to his eyelids.

The mouth had to be velvety red, and the chest, ample and uplifted. But the key to a successful transformation was less about breasts than buttocks. "What attracts men is a marked difference between waist size and hip size," Agent Mikhailovka had explained with authority, adding that the ideal ratio was approximately 7:10. After taking a few measurements with a tape, she unceremoniously stuffed the ultra-tight underwear that Maslo had been made to slip on and surveyed her handiwork while the members of the operational cell looked on approvingly. The makeup-wearing man of a moment ago had metamorphosed. Maslo himself had to agree: he was a splendid woman.

Luring the traitor to his hotel room was child's play. But as soon as the door clicked shut the double agent whipped out a straight razor. Maslo was overwhelmed with doubt: Was the man on to him? He soon understood that what the spy actually had in mind was to act out his sadistic fantasies with the defenceless woman he believed was standing in front of him. Maslo would never forget the panic in his adversary's eyes on realizing that he was dealing with a Russian agent. Maslo took his time finishing him off with his flawlessly manicured hands.

After that, whenever a mission called for a hundred kilos of muscle in the shape of woman who appeared to weigh half as much, they sent Maslo. The challenge spiced up his career. He was adept at fighting, hitting a target at twelve hundred metres, administering poison, driving cars, running computers; assassinations had become all but mundane for him. But doing it in drag changed everything.

He enjoyed creating effects, using perfumes, makeup, and curling irons to create the perfect smokescreen. And more than anything, he loved his voice. Maslo effortlessly found the octave that erased its gruffness and replaced it with a warm mellifluence that he unleashed on his targets. He sometimes amused himself by putting on various accents to add an exotic touch. He injected his Russian with sharp Germanic angles or the sensuality of the French socialists. In English, he became a quirky Australian woman or a frantic Italian. When he spoke German he stayed Russian. It was enough to fascinate most of his victims.

The dazzling redhead, the clever Asian, the mischievous babushka artfully carried out some twenty missions. Then the eighties swept over the Soviet empire, Gorbachev came to power, and the assignments grew less and less interesting. Maslo watched the Berlin Wall come down on the staticky television of a New York hotel room. You didn't need a Ph.D. in political science to figure out that yesterday's heroes would soon be public enemies. The lining of his travel bag concealed two passports that the KGB knew nothing about. Maslo closed his eyes and picked one. *Canada*, he read on the cover.

He had every reason not to go back to Montreal, which is why he decided to move there. When he arrived, he spent almost twenty-four hours on a little pilgrimage that took him from the waterfront grain silos to the Olympic Stadium and from the east-end refineries to the generous greenery of La Fontaine Park. Autumn was at hand, the ground was cold, and everything reminded him of Mila. Standing by the park's large, stinking pond, Maslo wept as if he'd been buried alive.

Fortunately, the semi-decrepit city was blessed with a tremendous energy that penetrated where neither the wind nor even the light could get in: gaps between buildings, cracks in the concrete, the depths of basements crowded with jobless people drunk on poetry and lust. This time around Maslo was free to take part in these festivities, admire the multicoloured facades, and stroll down the alleys overflowing with the organic commotion of lives in close proximity. For a lifelong traveller like Maslo, feeling at home anywhere had become an aptitude on a par with speaking many languages. In Montreal, this knack of his was hardly necessary. The city welcomed him with a wonderful insouciance.

He rented an apartment for a song, not far from the park and the bars in an area shared by students, junkies, homosexuals, and where he knew he would sleep soundly. When the winter storms swept in, the windowpanes rattled and the cold drafts nipped Maslo's big feet through his valenki slippers. He drank syrupy coffee that boiled his lips and made his hand tremble, and wolfed down gargantuan helpings of baked beans, a local dish that he was happy to have discovered. His days were spent reading, and in the evening he slipped on his tracksuit with the logo of the GUGB, an acronym that meant nothing to the rare passersby that he came across during his nighttime jogs.

Taking infinite precautions, he sent a coded letter to his sister and elderly mother. His sister wrote back that their mother no longer recognized anyone and that she herself was trying to forget the brother who had deserted the fatherland. He stopped writing letters to Russia altogether.

When spring came he moved to a new place on Ontario Street located above a grocer's fruit stall that released the first fragrances of life in May and where the customers' voices sent out a sunny spray of local accents. On a few occasions, when he extended his walks to the posh avenues of Outremont, he thought he'd recognized Mila, that Romansh killer's gait of hers and the categorical clack of her heels on concrete. But he pulled himself together. He had to keep the visions at bay if he was to stay sane in this city where he'd once found love and very quickly lost it again.

The idea occurred to Maslo one summer night while he was on his way back from a run along the riverbank. The sweat was literally pouring off him and as he wiped his brow going up Visitation Street he heard bursts of laughter coming from a hole in the wall. Taken aback, he edged his dripping head into the doorway and saw a woman as long as a knife wearing an extravagant orange wig. She was whispering the unintelligible words of a song that, judging from the audience's excitement, was obviously risqué. He watched the show from the sidewalk until the transvestite called out to him. "Hey, you there! The gorilla! If you want to listen you have to pay!" Getting no reaction from him, the lady stepped down from the stage and crossed the room, threading her way through the tables, the pastel cocktails and curly heads of hair, and then let fly at him with missiles drawn from her capacious bra. Maslo slowly retreated.

The next evening his preparations took forever. He hadn't touched his cosmetic kit for a long time, and he had never had to deal with such sultry weather. The foundation seemed to dissolve as soon as he applied it, and the mascara ran as if he were bawling his eyes out. He therefore decided to go with minimalist makeup, based on a few strokes of blush. A magnificent blond wig and a sequin dress rounded out the illusion. When he stepped outside, the luminous music that accompanied him as soon as he transformed into a woman took over.

The words on the board at the entrance to the bar made him smile: "Open Mic." Neither the barman nor the drag queen seemed to recognize him from the night before. So Maslo confidently pulled a cigarette case from his décolleté and asked for a light, his voice freighted with Russian ornamentation. The waiter was intrigued and brought a flame close to his face. Maslo turned toward the fan and blew smoke into the airstream with a fierce pout. The people seated at the tables shot admiring glances his way. The former spy smiled inwardly. He was gorgeous and he knew it.

The evening began with an Édith Piaf number rendered by a devoted but sour voice. A duo made up of twins, one white, the other black, performed a languid tango. Then Romy Bruchési tickled the house with a few smutty jokes. Toward one in the morning, when the crowd's drunkenness was at its peak, Maslo slid off his barstool and took a few steps, instantly lighting up the room with the flash of his sequins.

He seized the microphone and let his gaze settle heavy and hard on the audience until they fell silent. Taking a deep breath of stale air, he intoned the opening notes of "Ochi chyornye," Dark Eyes, the most famous and torrid song ever to come out of torrid Russia. During the few minutes of his rendition, no one breathed, no one laughed, cigarettes burned down to the fingers that held them. Maslo's voice stirred the long-dead loves of these night owls, their fleeting passions, their unfinished grieving. When the final notes died out on his lips, the audience burst into applause.

"Your name! What's your name?" someone shouted. Maslo turned and answered solemnly, "Victoria Volga." The applause erupted again, and as she left the stage she let the mic drop behind her.

Two weeks were all it took for Victoria Volga to get her own billing at the cabaret. She was given a Thursday booking, which suited her perfectly: not a slow midweek slot but not a crazy weekend night either. The hungry anticipation of approaching leisure time, but also the despair of an ordinary day. Much of the cabaret's clientele was made up of women trapped in men's bodies, businessmen, truckers, family men who came to get a little breath of oxygen before diving back into the airless world where they had built themselves small, unbearable prisons. These poor souls who dreamed of another life rubbed shoulders with happily open homosexuals tanking up before the night really took off in the Gay Village, and with matrons who came from as far away as the North Shore suburbs to have some fun mixing with queens who understood them better than their sisters, neighbours, or husbands.

Victoria Volga clashed like a gong in this company. No barnyard humour for this stoic Soviet, just emotions like molten lava, just the great soul of Russia flowing from her lips and into the patrons' drinking glasses. Thanks to a repertoire made relatively exotic by the Iron Curtain, she offered something unique, and the bar paid for her originality in hard cash. By topping up her Thursday earnings with a few nights blending cocktails behind the counter she no longer had to dip into her savings to get by. She had a job.

She bought her outfits at second-hand stores on Mont-Royal Avenue and church basements in the upscale neighbourhoods. Soon her male wardrobe seemed inadequate to her, so even on her days off she continued to wear tight skirts and plush sweaters, close-fitting slacks, and flamboyant blouses.

The one thing that disrupted the harmony of her daily life was the recurring apparition of Mila. Amid the frenzy of last call, just when Victoria was about to launch into "Kalinka," Mila's face would emerge at the far end of the room, her austere, graceful features, her eyes as black as a nine-millimetre barrel. Sometimes Victoria didn't actually see her but felt the harsh judgment of her former lover, who surely would have found her grotesque tricked out this way. Whenever this happened, she shut her eyes so tightly her false eyelashes were in peril of flying off, spread her arms wide, and began to sing; Mila disappeared and Victoria drove the hallucination out of her thoughts.

As predicted, the USSR fell apart, and the former agent followed every stage of its disintegration, from the Moscow putsch to the establishment of the Commonwealth of Independent States. She would have laughed at the suggestion that those dirges so dear to the Red Army Choir helped her cope with her sense of loss. Still, there was no denying that since going into exile she had never felt so Russian. She had reshaped herself according to an absolute cliché, but one that she inhabited so wholeheartedly as to make it convincing.

The winters marched past, closely flanked by autumns and springs that ushered in the fleeting summers when Montreal stewed like a potful of soup. Her face showed one or two new wrinkles, she quit smoking three times only to start again, and slept with a few women, mothers or younger women in search of new continents. Once a year she returned to the bleak maze of the east-end refineries. At the spot where Mila had died, an oil stain stubbornly persisted. Killing the woman she loved so deeply had given her a reason to die, and this had infused her undercover work with a kind of recklessness. It remained the pivotal moment of her life, even now. But she no longer wished to die. She wanted to go back to the scenes of the worst mission ever assigned to her and to experience, with all the ambivalence of her body, the sort of man she once was. Hard, obedient, and stupid. Had Maslo been slower to act, Mila surely would have killed him first.

It was on the day of that anniversary that she met Mila again. Victoria was down on one knee, deep in meditation, when she felt a stab in her back, in the exact spot where the bullet that killed Mila had exited after boring a hole through her heart. The point was so precise that at first

Victoria thought she was dreaming. Then she heard the hard heels striking the asphalt behind her and quickly realized that the apparitions of her former lover had not been mirages. She turned around.

"I may have killed you, Mila d'Eon, but I didn't shoot you in the back."

"Well, I have. I shoot people in the back. And you didn't kill me."

"Obviously not."

"You, on the other hand, have about three minutes left before lethal paralysis sets in."

Mila yanked a dart out of Victoria's back and handed it to her. Victoria calmly considered the originality of the method adopted to eliminate her.

"My just deserts."

"It's not what you think. I'm not after revenge."

"Oh, really?"

Mila stepped closer and angrily clutched Victoria's blond hair.

"I want to punish you for being so completely ridiculous!"

She flung the wig far away, pulled Victoria near to her, and planted a brutal kiss on her lips.

Despite being one of the most closely watched places on Montreal Island, the refinery district was deserted. Unseen, Mila and Victoria made love savagely. Once they'd put their clothes back on, Victoria was amused to see the streaks of rouge she'd left on Mila's neck.

"Looks like I'm not about to die."

"Of course not. There was nothing but lemon juice on the dart."

"I love you, Mila."

Mila gave her a stern look and then picked up her Hermès bag, which held—Victoria hadn't doubted it for even a second—a Glock and enough poison to slay a regiment. She disappeared among the storage tanks and Victoria headed back with the sense that the order of the world had just been overturned. The refinery lights blinked in the evening moonscape. In a little while it would be her turn to step up to the mic.

She spent many feverish hours desperately looking for Mila. She scoured the city and combed through the most arcane records trying to track her down. Recovering her old reflexes, she followed every possible trail, from newspaper archives to political organizations, from shooting clubs to the courthouse clerk. At wit's end, she even inquired at the consulate of Russia, one of the four countries of which Mila was a citizen. Speaking with a flawless Québécois accent, Victoria explained to the official that she was looking for a former tenant who had decamped without paying her rent.

"She told me she was Russian. Her name is Mila d'Eon."

At this, the sad-eyed bureaucrat stopped scanning the sports page and looked up at her.

"How long was this woman a tenant of yours?"

"I'm not sure . . . a few months."

"And she said her name was Mila d'Eon?"

"Yes. I'd like to know if she's still in the country. If there's a way to get the money she owes me."

"Excuse me for a moment."

The man went out of the office. Squirming in her chair, Victoria waited for what seemed like an eternity. Since her defection she had never been so close to her former bosses. It made her nervous. When the functionary came back he looked Victoria straight in the eye.

"The woman you're looking for has indeed been reported missing, Madame Tremblay. And it would be best if your search ended here and now."

He had spoken in Russian, his voice perfectly calm, articulating the words "Madame Tremblay" a little more slowly than the rest. Victoria nodded and cautiously made for the exit riddled with multiple lenses that recorded each of her movements.

That afternoon she took a leave of absence, packed her belongings, and changed her address. Having discarded her blond wigs, she turned into a brunette and got rid of everything that had been left over from her former life. Using her makeup kit, she fashioned a new face for herself, more subtle and low-key, in keeping with what she needed to become: an inconspicuous woman. As she applied a second layer of foundation she studied her reflection in the mirror, trying to locate among her features the interior enemy that had made her life such a failure.

After a while she went back to the cabaret burdened with her obsession and a broken heart. She would gladly have given up her now thoroughly joyless job, if not for the hope of seeing Mila's ruthless pout poking out among the audience. Shunning the stage, she spent her nights behind the bar surveying the crowd in search of a sign. Mila's shadow was omnipresent, pervasive, toxic.

The anxiety made Victoria's muscles wither and her face sag. She even seemed to grow shorter; her feet shrank inside her cheap shoes. Her voice went up to unfamiliar heights, and her body hair became increasingly sparse. Victoria was wholly preoccupied with her quest and didn't notice these changes right away. But one day, as she was coming back after a stroll around La Fontaine Park, she felt it. The difference. An alteration at once subtle and radical lashing the pivotal centre of her body. She raced home in disbelief, but her mirror confirmed the spectacular transmogrification: in the place that just yesterday had held the last vestiges of the man he had been, there were female genitals like all those she had known, endowed with the various curves, dimples, and smiles that made them unique. On her chest, the pectoral muscles had given way to tired but proud breasts, and her sides had acquired new contours that narrowed her waistline. Like a planet that changes its axis, her body had tipped over.

She settled into her new anatomical geography without talking about it to anyone, happy just to inhabit the structure that had taken shape for her. But at the cabaret her colleagues sensed the transformation, and most of them reacted to this intuition with instinctive scorn, as if her new-found authenticity somehow discredited her. What was valued in this community was the fact of being both one and the other, of being midway, of never arriving anywhere. Her shift had placed her in a camp from which there was no way out.

This is when Mila decided to resurface. One Tuesday, while Victoria was watching the rerun of Julia Alexandrovna Kourotchkina's triumph at the Miss World pageant on her little TV, the telephone rang with a miraculous chime. There was an unusual note of tenderness in Mila's voice as she once again turned the universe upside down.

"You're a father, Maslo."

Victoria was speechless for almost a minute, so Mila repeated the message until it found its way from the heart to the head.

"But how?!"

"The usual way."

"Where are you?"

"We're at the hospital. Come."

The wind from the west was almost a gale, making each step a struggle, as in a dream where everything holds you back. At the intersections, the red held the other traffic lights hostage for hours. An endless stream of buses barred her way; road closures forced her to take unimaginable detours. The blood pounded in her temples; a minuscule second heart pulsed in her body. She was a father. Father and mother at the same time. She was about to become heaven and earth to a tiny human being that Mila, though full of resentment, had brought into the world. Let the wind blow; she was an arrow determined to fly north.

The hospital loomed up on the mountainside like a Russian ballad. Victoria headed toward Pavilion F, the Women's Pavilion, where lives began between women's legs, were greeted with women's hands and rocked by women who knew the secrets of all women. Victoria approached the entrance with the impression of arriving at a temple. But before she could touch the doorhandle she was hailed by a whistle. Her whole skin shuddered. She recognized this sound from another era. It was the signal she and Mila had agreed on to find each other in the darkness and chaos. Victoria answered, blowing between her lip and her incisors, and then started up the road that plunged into the mountain, unsurprised that her beloved had chosen to wait for her in the woods rather than some yellowish room. In a thousand ways, Mila d'Eon belonged more to the forest than to civilization.

She found herself under the canopy of a massive tree. The ground was carpeted with apples. Mila, dressed in a linen blanket, with her hair down, was smiling. "Unarmed," Victoria thought. She could not keep from hugging her, from caressing her, from doing the things that usually annoyed Mila but that she seemed to accept today.

"I needed to get some air, so I waited for you here."

"Where's our child?"

"Sleeping. I'll take you in a few moments."

"Is he all right?"

"Yes."

"Is it a girl? A boy?"

Mila shook her head, and Victoria realized she'd never seen her this way, her hair floating in the wind. Like the rest of her soul, Mila always kept her hair tightly tied, close against her skull, impossible to grab in a fight or when making love. She took a long time to reply and looked Victoria up and down with a brutal, penetrating gaze that seemed to see through her clothes. She shrugged as if none of this mattered.

"A boy."

"A boy," Victoria repeated.

Mila averted her eyes. The apple tree was enormous, evidently very old. Older perhaps than all this, these buildings, these births, these unfathomable loves. Planted by a poor settler with a sweet tooth. The ground seemed to be made of apples that rolled underfoot.

"Have you chosen a name?"

Mila shook her head slowly with a tender look, which suddenly turned fierce. The wind came up.

"We'll find one together," Victoria said.

"Yes."

Victoria breathed in and her chest filled with all-new confidence. She leaned down to pick up an apple and rubbed it on her jacket. Mila gave her a gentle smile.

"No, not that one. It's pitted."

She handed her a different apple, smaller and redder, as if the essence of all the other apples had been instilled in it.

"This one. Here."

Victoria opened her mouth and bit into the fruit, which gave out an almost gleeful crunch. She instantly felt the darkness swooping down. She barely had time to hear the sound, to the east of her body, of footsteps receding.

Victoria Kumari

I WAS A SAINT. An icon, an idol. People came from everywhere to worship me, to smother me in smoke, fragrant herbs, and orange peels. I was a living goddess. I was a Kumari.

For seven years, my feet never touched the ground. My meals were brought to my bed, I was carried to my bath, transported to the temple, and I floated over everything like a beam of light. My life was a network of triangles, stars, and crosses that I was able to decipher. The gods are all-knowing; I was exempted from learning. The gods have no one to appeal to; I did not have to pray. I was red, I was gold, with a formidable eye in the middle of my brow.

I can still recall the sound that set everything in motion. The dry clink of a tooth dropping into an empty bowl. My mother wept. I thought I'd done something wrong. The first of my teeth to fall out. But my mother wept for joy. In my memory, it rained milk teeth all over Montreal. Actually, it may have snowed—it makes no difference. That day, the tall chimneys, the decontamination tanks, the doomed districts, the rickety hovels, all became sacred. I closed my eyes for seven years and saw everything.

When the perfect little girl loses her first milk tooth, she is of an age to be chosen. The holy men of the Great All arrive—lamas, cardinals, astrologers, ulema—and examine her mouth, arms, hair, on the lookout for hidden flaws. Then they search her skin for the mark of the goddess Akna. When they find it, they smile and draw the Eternal Eye on her forehead. My skull was filled with warmth while they made their drawing. That is how, in a cloud of charcoal and cayenne, I learned that my life was about to change. Again my mother wept.

After that, I became the one they had chosen. Because Akna, the goddess I incarnated, is fearless, they made me spend a night in a room full of animal heads, with the reek of hooves and missing skins, the stench of blood, and flies all around. I did not cry. In the morning they declared that I possessed the bravery of the saints. They purified me, the embers, the ardent bells, the priests' hands coated with an oil that penetrated my skin like a serpent's tongue. They danced. I closed my two eyes and opened the third.

I beheld the gold, the cloths, the sculpted altars inside the palace of the Zenith. Outside, the city was no longer grey, but golden. Its sparkling soot and dust revealed its modest illuminations through the ruins and slums. In the distance, the sacred mountain greeted me. What once had frightened me, I now dominated. I was mistress of the desperate and the survivors. During my appearances at the window I looked out at the faithful and did my best to bestow my grace upon them. I would have preferred to give my compassion to these poor devotees, who laid their misery and miscarriages at my feet. But the White Priest repeatedly cautioned me: pity is the grace of mortals. The grace of the gods is serenity.

I was little, but I was not a child anymore. Thus, it behooved me not to smile, shout, or play. This was difficult. At first, I amused myself by blowing on the confetti strewn over the ground, making them race each other, yellow against pink, blue pulls ahead of black. Or I imagined I was the one who determined the movements of the shadows thrown up from the courtyard onto my window. When I wanted to see them dance, they danced. If I wished for them to lie flat, they dropped down. Gradually, though, I lost the taste for such games, at once too simple and too complicated. What's more, they were false. My head filled with light. The shadows ceased to exist.

The Kumaris appeared a very long time ago, before the era of the Great All, before the Plague that had preceded it. The world was then a constellation of villages and families, and the water was still pristine and pure. At the time, Akna was the friend of a very powerful king. When he betrayed her, she went to hide among the little girls of his kingdom, condemning the king, generation after generation, to find the one possessed of divinity. When the world was unified, the guardians of tradition migrated here, ready to discover the goddesses hidden among the white multitudes of our continent. But only after the Plague, when chaos took root, did the survivors turn to the power of the Kumaris. Since then, each decade brings a new little girl to be venerated.

The faithful would come on foot from the four corners of the island to supplicate me. The women entreated me to end the cycle of stillborn babies, to stop the blood or make it come back when it was spent. They wished for happy births, twins, triplets, the litters of tigresses. The young men wanted me to bless their makeshift weapons and tools; the old men prayed for water, meat, a dry bed where they might put their final illnesses to sleep. If I cried, laughed, shouted, or yawned; if I turned my head, sneezed, rubbed my eyes, hiccoughed, or if my stomach gurgled, the faithful concluded that their death was imminent, that they would lose their children, that everything they owned would be taken from them and their humble dwellings burned down. I strived to say still. When I failed, the faithful would go away tearing their hair out.

I missed my mother at first. The statues of Krishna, Calvin, and Nostradamus that stood in my room looked at me with stern expressions. I swallowed my tears. My father and my brother sometimes came to visit. They weren't permitted to share my meals or sleep in the palace of the Zenith. I kept from crying in their presence too. I didn't want them to leave under unfavourable auspices. One day I presented them with a gift, a piece of paper that a servant had delicately folded into the shape of a bird for me. They accepted it with a bow. Later, I saw them place it on an altar before crossing the central square like strangers.

From time to time, irreverent individuals would wave to me like old friends. They expected me to wave back. They stayed rooted under my window while pilgrims looked daggers at them; they would point at my Eternal Eye and then leave. The goddess in me wanted to strike them down, to bring them closer, embrace them, and eat their heads. Once, on a stormy night, I waited to be alone, took an apple from the fruit bowl, and flung it at the statue of the Destroyer. The apple shattered against the god's stomach. The next day Montreal was struck by an earthquake and what remained of the old hospital was engulfed.

I was frightened the day I felt two hard bumps push their way through my chest. It was painful, and it was ugly. My eldest servant, the one who bathed and perfumed me when I awoke, explained that these were chrysanthemum buds on the verge of bursting open to light the world. At night I looked under my nightgown, worried I might miss their opening. It would have given me nightmares, had I not stopped dreaming the day I lost my first tooth.

It was the blood, as always, that put an end to it all. One night as I was undressing, I discovered a dark red trickle on my thigh. The servants were aghast and bowed before backing out of the room. For the first time in seven years I remained alone and naked, with no one to dress me and accompany me to my bed. I clumsily put on my clothes, I had almost forgotten how. I stayed on my seat, waiting for them to come back and carry me across the room. An eternity went by. I realized I was no longer a Kumari. The goddess had left my body along with those first drops of blood.

I stood up and set my foot down on the ground, which was oddly cold and rough. I made my way to my bed as best I could. My legs were unable to carry me. My head was unable to think. I slept one last time in the palace of Zenith, with the Destroyer and his thousand laughing mouths. The next day the White Priest escorted me to my parents' house. Outside, I opened my eyes wider than wide. I had put out of my mind the violence in the streets, the smell of roasted pigeon, the cries of the vendors, and the sores of the stray dogs. I had forgotten the magnitude of the prayer, when the chants filled the buildings and the brow of every passerby. My Eternal Eye had been erased, I was dressed in grey, and no one recognized me.

My mother had died five years earlier. I didn't know. My father had chosen not to disturb the goddess with such details, and, besides, the priests had forbidden him from telling me. My brother had left home to go defend the borders along with other young men who would never come back. The house was cramped and crooked and the food was stale. The little shoes my father had sewn for my return did not fit. I had very large feet. Feet that could no longer walk straight.

My father now worked as a fisherman. He would go out on the oily river for weeks at a time, sailing with two or three stalwarts until the water could not be plumbed, where the fish swim joylessly, waiting to be caught and sold to the rich in Montreal. He came home reeking from head to toe, his eyes still full of terrifying storms and aquatic monsters; he rested for a few days before putting out to sea again.

While he was away, I nibbled on nuts and overripe fruits, I watched the drab sun cross the city from east to west, I slept amid the howling of lost dogs. The sacred matter that had occupied the inside of my head had scattered and not been replaced. I twisted bits of thread, pretending to sew clothes without any idea of how to make them; I kept the fire going, hard put to accept the idea that it no longer bent to my will, that epidemics came and went at the command of another goddess. In truth, I was at loose ends. My father left me enough money to keep me from begging. I could neither read nor dance. I didn't know anyone. Men gave me wide berth because whoever married a former Kumari was struck down within a year. Through the window I watched the young lovers and the thieves loitering in front of our house.

One winter, my father did not return. The fishing season was drawing to a close, and the sailors came back covered with frostbite and completely cloaked in green plastic. My father was not among them. I did not know how to find him, whom to ask. I began to search for him at all the piers, stumbling whenever I tried to step over a fish head. Part of me was horrified at the thought of treading the ground; I was convinced that the earth would gobble up the soles of my feet through my thin shoes. I stopped at each vessel and said my father's name, to no avail. No one had heard of him. The snow set in and obliterated all traces. There was nothing I could do anymore.

Miniature temples were aflame on every square, lighting up the cold, enveloping the passersby in their scents and then gently releasing them when they were done praying. Like everyone else, I stopped there briefly, joining my hands together in front of my brow. But on one particularly harsh December morning, I found myself on my knees, my shins sunk into the frozen mud, bowing to a saint with indistinct features. Tears were streaming down my cheeks although I was not sad.

I worshipped for an hour, maybe more, in the grip of that venerable vise. Suddenly, a peppery heat radiated over my forehead. I broke off my meditation and turned around. Before me stood a Sage, barefoot in the snow, wearing only a simple sheet, her braid floating on the cold wind. She laughed as she drew an indiscernible symbol between my eyebrows. She placed her large, bony hand on my head and looked at me first with her blue eye, then with her green eye.

"Little Kumari, you have not lost the divine. The gods inhabit all things, all creatures. Your skull is still warm. You are a step away from the blessed renouncement. You know where to go."

She bent down before me. She was right. I knew. The Sage touched her chin by way of a greeting. I stayed on my knees in front of the now derisory altar. I, too, laughed. My heart spread out to every part of my body. I stood up, located north, and set off. I was an arrow, patient and straight.

I quickly learned the stride of true walkers, of wanderers and saints, those who move swiftly without ever hurrying. My legs grew long and powerful. I crossed the city and its winding streets. Along the way I came across men pulling heavy carts laden with objects found in the unfathomable crusts of civilization. I saw children, little girls with tiny truths suspended in their eyes, and sulking boys who one day would find enlightenment. Women washing their hair in icy streams, caring for the beauty that had been entrusted to them while at the same time letting it drift away. Each of my steps slipped another loop onto the long prayer that I dedicated to them. They were in me, and I poured myself into them.

Then a blizzard blew in. The mountain loomed more imperious, its reign grew jealous. But the trails I took had been there for centuries, blazed by people who had died for me long before I was born. The steepest slopes did not leave me breathless; the abrupt descents did not compel me to run. I was slow and sedulous and I covered the distances in giant strides. The snow piled up swiftly. At times my legs were buried to mid-thigh; the winds rushed to meet me head-on, but I felt neither suffering nor hardship. I advanced without needing to rest or eat. My journey was a meditation, and my body, my limbs, my bones, my blood resonated with one lone, long syllable.

I climbed until I heard the sound of the drum. The gods were close. I examined the rock face. An outcrop formed a modest grotto surrounded by soft-shaped crevices. I sat down. The snow did not reach me even though it was within reach. I did not feel the wind, yet it too blew the same long syllable. No living thing stood before me, only a frail city, only a prayer.

All saints belong to a place. They discover it, settle in there, live there, and when they die the place takes their name; centuries on, pilgrims and inhabitants remember them and point them out, drawing nourishment from the calm that emanates from them. This was a perfect spot, neither too high, nor too low, nor too hard, nor too easy. I shut my eyes.

Victoria in Time

SHE WAS THE KIND of woman whose beauty serves as a rudder or, more exactly, a keel. Their fate becomes a compound of the desires of others, of those who attempt to get closer to them with all sorts of offerings. Half-blind to this situation, such women advance, take, enjoy, discard, and forget so easily, never wondering about the inner workings of that ease.

Already as a little girl, Victoria was entitled to special consideration. She was scolded less than her siblings. She was allowed to stay up later, go barefoot, and snack between meals. Without even realizing it, her teachers would give her higher marks. Shopkeepers treated her to so many sweets that for a long time she believed that candy was essential and free, like water. Staring into empty space, she would suck on the sweets while the sugar spread inside her. Then, one day, puberty overtook her body and she was borne away toward empires that succumbed even before she could name them.

She was a fashion model, a dancer, and had starred in four films, her tranquil face evincing in a single quiver the whole range of human emotions. She sang with famous musicians, and her voice, thin but true, became the soundtrack of a generation. She was recruited by a major news network and supplied the entire planet with its daily dose of news, gently floating above wars and famines with her spellbound audience in tow.

Luxurious clothes, perfumes, fine wines and food as sublime as ether, the most exquisite works of art—all of it came to her like little animals scurrying toward her unbidden. She lived in sumptuous houses, apartments, or country estates with fur-lined walls at the heart of which her own heart pulsed, pink, slow, and sound. She travelled the world and outer space, and cast her placid gaze on everything. She was hardly aware of being asleep, and shifted from waking to sleeping and from sleeping to waking with the same fluidity as the air going in and out of her lungs.

There was love, of course, a burning problem that she had never brought to heel. Passions and pledges flowed in her direction, but all the men who passed through her life went insane. They crumbled in her hands like little chunks of dry bread, crying for their mothers as soon as she touched them. Some tried to shut her in and thus imprison her unbearable beauty. Others, men for whom no woman is deserving of kindness, treated her with a blend of contempt and brute desire. Victoria handled all of them with equanimity. She slipped through their fingers and returned to her sphere, her perfect wholeness.

She rarely laughed, ate without appetite, drank without getting drunk, and walked the way others skate. That stride took her to the centre of summit meetings, where she acted as a balm on the strained relations between world powers. She was the one who rang the opening of stock markets, who lit the Olympic flames, who greeted the first hour of the first day of every new year and kissed the astronauts on their return from distant planets.

So it was to be expected, once the reputed firm Eon & Eon had put the finishing touches on their machine, that they should choose Victoria for its maiden voyage. Who else could they have invited to be the ambassador of the twenty-fifth century? The media's mighty synthetic heart beat in time with the preparations, broadcasting Victoria's voice far and wide as she discussed her forthcoming journey like someone heading to the beach. In fact, nothing about this new venture frightened her. The machine had been tested, Victoria had absolute faith in the scientists who had designed it, and she would be dealing with a reasonably advanced epoch. She had nothing to fear.

The departure was set to coincide with her birthday. There were banners everywhere emblazoned with her picture and the words *VICTORIA, THE FIRST TIME-TRAVELLER*. A group of protesters had gathered in front of the laboratory to voice their opposition to the voyage on the grounds that by visiting the twentieth century Victoria might perturb the course of history. It would be better, the malcontents argued, to send someone who looked ordinary and could go unnoticed among the masses of that period. Victoria risked turning the bygone society topsy-turvy, endangering thousands of births, delaying suicides, befuddling poets and politicians. But a change of plan was now out of the question. Victoria was to be propelled into the past like a glorious arrow shot toward the north of History.

The capsule was as cozy as a nicely brooded egg yolk. Victoria installed herself in a throne-like seat. Enthralled technicians checked the machine's calibrations one last time to make sure their precious pioneer would not end up locked in a cosmic gap for all eternity. In every corner of the earth and throughout the colonies, among the last of the Bedouins and the most reclusive hermits, those who did not follow every second of the great departure were rare indeed. Victoria's casual wave would become an iconic image. She had achieved immortality.

The capsule was launched and a mild fatigue swept over her. She could have dozed off in that very intimate cabin transported by the rivers of time. Her breathing grew deeper, deeper still, and weaker. Suddenly, Victoria found herself drenched. Groping around her she realized that she was floating in a warm, dark liquid. She took a few moments to indulge in that sensation, and when she sensed there would be no more movement she pressed gently against the wall of her vessel. The hatch creaked open and Victoria rose to her feet.

The room was dark and filled with soothing sounds. Looking down, she saw that the instruments, the seat, even the water that had been in the cabin a few moments ago, had vanished. Victoria shrugged and stepped out of the cabin to search for an exit. It appeared of its own accord when a door opened for a woman in white.

"You're already dressed? Your session isn't over. You have the use of the float tank for a full hour."

Victoria eyed her calmly. She was keen to go out and explore the twentieth century. She waited to be allowed to pass; instead, the woman pushed a switch that brought the lights up.

"You're soaking! Didn't someone tell you to take your clothes off before getting in?"

Elbowing Victoria aside, the lady went over to the tank.

"There's no water? What happened?"

"I don't know," Victoria replied and went out.

The corridor was suffused with a hazy brightness. Still dripping wet, Victoria imprinted the floor with little bluish puddles as she proceeded down the passageway. A majestic mahogany staircase took her to the ground floor, where large windows finally let her feast her eyes on the old earth-bound cars and people going by in archaic clothes. Something settled in Victoria's gut like a fallen flower petal, a certainty, a conclusion. She had done it.

Ignoring her sopping clothes and hair, she headed toward the door, ready to glide out into the windy streets. But she was intercepted by the woman who had greeted her.

"Madame! Madame! You can't just leave like this."

"It's okay, it's not very cold outside, is it?"

"What's going on?" a man behind an oak desk wanted to know.

"This lady went in with all her clothes on," the employee explained. "Not only that but she somehow drained the tank!"

Victoria turned slowly toward the man. He studied her unsmilingly. Then he screwed his face up in an ugly frown. She shuddered.

"I'm sorry, but I'm not to blame," she said.

"The fibres foul up our tanks. You'll have to pay for the cost of cleaning it up," the man declared in a sinister tone of voice.

As she had never been involved in a confrontation like this, Victoria, unlike ordinary people, lacked the subtlety of verbal jousting. She took a chance and fell back on an old classic.

"Fuck you!"

Once outside, she ran for a while, covering several city blocks with loping, fluid strides; she passed rows of corkscrew staircases and turned down right-angled streets. When she finally stopped, she was somewhat drier; she didn't recognize anything around her. She entered a random café.

The organizers of the voyage had given Victoria a small sum of period currency so she would not have to worry about getting by during the first weeks. Naturally, the banknotes were counterfeit, but the forgery was undetectable. In any case, Victoria, who had never paid for a thing in her life, doubted that the money would be necessary. But she liked the rustle of the small bills in her pocket, the coarse yet greasy sensation of the wad of cash on her fingers.

The place was packed and stifling. The crowd brushed against Victoria's sides, rough hands touched her elbows. Unfazed, she focused her attention on the server, who finally stopped to tell her, without batting an eye, that she would have to wait at least twenty minutes for a table. Victoria smiled incredulously at the young man. He gazed back at her for a few seconds with the same quizzical look.

"Listen, we're swamped right now. Wait there if you'd like something to eat, otherwise, you'll have to move out of the way."

Victoria, bewildered, burst out laughing, and the cascade of laughter took her by surprise. She paused to consider this sensation, to examine its tiny mechanism, and then left the restaurant. Rush-hour Montreal rumbled past, grey and lucent. There were decisions to be made, actions to be initiated, but until late into the evening all she could do was walk, hypnotized by a bus, distracted by the wail of a siren, drawn down an avenue by a trash collector's movements, captivated by the intricacy of a wrought iron balcony.

What interrupted her wandering was hunger, a sharp, red hunger that pierced her stomach with a fury she had never known. In a panic, she dashed into an eatery and wolfed down a rubbery pizza that rammed into her belly like a piledriver. Replete and exhausted, with a strange hum filling her ears, she made her way to a hotel. The noise swelled when she stepped into her modest room, and she had to duck her head down in the bathwater to silence it.

The next day she continued to ramble through the streets. Everything fascinated her: the cracked concrete, the parks and their majestic trees, the chemical-coloured clothes, the grisly stench of household garbage, the roar of the trucks. There was something seductive about this prodigal abundance. Downtown, the music spilling out of the shops made her stumble at every street corner. She spotted the building that the organizers of the voyage had indicated. Inside, she watched the office workers getting into and out of an elevator. The car emitted a worrisome squeal each time it went up. Shaking her head, she decided to take the stairs.

Her lungs were burning by the time she reached the eighteenth floor. After going around in circles, she eventually found the office of *La Perle*, a gossip magazine whose past issues were lovingly stored in the archives of the Eon & Eon company. Still in a sweat, she dictated to the clerk the wording of an advertisement to be published the following week. *GREAT TRAVELLER HAS LANDED. VICTORIA SEARCHES FOR LOST TIME.* The clerk noted down the message without looking up or asking any questions, never suspecting that the words he was writing on the form were intended for women and men whose great-grandparents had not yet been born.

With this detail out of the way, Victoria located the streets where the fashionable restaurants and boutiques were concentrated. Feeling both at home and a stranger in this antiquated luxury, she dined on duck legs and bought a pair of suede leather boots. Stuffed with flesh and shod in animal hide, she continued to roam the city. Actually, the terms of her mission were exceedingly broad. She simply had been told to leave, live for a while in 1999, and come back whenever she felt the need. The primary goal was to test the device that made it possible to travel from one epoch to another. Everything else was a fog that Victoria was free to navigate as she saw fit.

After what seemed like an endless day, sleep still eluded her. At around two a.m. she realized what the matter was and undressed. Ever since she had been a teenager this was how she'd filled her idle hours. When she was alone, her nudity took on a new meaning. In the presence of others she attracted every particle of attention and sucked up all the ambient energy. But in an empty room, this body of hers was no more than a body that she could caress and listen to, one that breathed through every pore. Victoria stroked her skin, her hair, massaged the small muscles of her feet, hefted the perfect orbs of her chest. She was a loaf of bread, a tree, a heavy and friendly bolt of cloth. Yet something was not right. Something was off, didn't add up. A worried frown creased her brow. What if she had lost something during the voyage? What if her molecules had not reassembled correctly?

Victoria rarely dwelt on her reflection. Her image didn't interest her. She *was*; the stability of her figure and its finer aspects were enough for her. She used mirrors only to make sure her hair was not out of place or to inspect her skin, which very occasionally indulged in a mild itch. Still naked, hardly bothered by the few degrees of heat that her room lacked, she stepped in front of the mirror and scrutinized herself. Her arms were the same. The shape of her eyes was unchanged. Her buttocks had withstood the journey, and her legs were as streamlined as ever. Everything was in its proper place, and yet the dissonance persisted.

All through her rides on the buses, in the Metro, in wild taxis, and as she walked along the boulevards and past the old stone buildings, the malaise clung to her like an urge to cough. It took her a while to discover the source of this distress. It was neither the place nor the period but the inhabitants or, rather, the way they behaved toward her. The gaze of others had become a cloak that enveloped her at every moment of her life. But since her arrival in the twentieth century, no one had looked at her for more than a few seconds. She had received just a few passing glances, which stung more than they comforted.

She therefore began to stare at people, to study them as never before. Incapable of initiating a discussion with a stranger, she sat down on a park bench, picked out a passerby and fixed her eyes on that person, determined not to look away until they felt the weight of her gaze, turned around, took the first step, and from that first step a conversation, a journey, an odyssey, possible worlds would ensue. But all she managed to do was to prompt a few businessmen to hurry away and make a small child cry.

Despite her diet of heavy foods rich in animal fat, she felt constantly hungry and cold. She bought clothes made of synthetic fibres but they did not keep her warm. Eager to restore her body's lost balance, she haunted spas, saunas, and meditation centres, yet the peace of mind she sought slipped through her fingers. It was an expensive lifestyle, and her nest egg shrank. Victoria dreamed of finding a treasure chest or a sack full of gold; she thought so hard about it that she was almost disappointed when the bonanza failed to materialize. She needed to find work, to offer an employer her intangible, unverifiable experience. But she had no clue where to begin, how to describe her qualifications, how to display them. She was caught in the jaws of a vise, where her ideas fizzled out even before they could come to light.

When she was down to her last coins, the hotel manager unceremoniously showed her the door. November descended on the city like salt on a wound. Victoria put on all of her outfits in successive layers and left the building. She walked for hours, distraught and grimacing in the raw wind. For the first time in her life she wanted to be somewhere else. Before setting out for the twentieth century she had been told, "To come back, all you need to do is to return to the exact spot where you first arrived." She headed toward the northern part of the city.

The man in charge of the relaxation centre seemed not to recognize the unkempt woman standing in front of him in a polyester spacesuit.

"Can I help you?"

"I'd like . . . hmm . . . a flotation tank, please."

"There's nothing free right now."

"Well, can I have an appointment for another day?"

The man gave her an unfriendly pout as he looked her up and down.

"I'm afraid we're booked up," he said without even peeking at his schedule. "There's nothing available."

Victoria appeared disheartened as she made for the exit. When she was certain no one was watching her she spun around and stole over to the stairs leading to the room where she had emerged from her capsule. The layers of clothing slowed her progress, but she absolutely had to reach the second floor.

She had made it to the fourth step when she was caught. A security guard grabbed her and shouted: "Don't resist, ma'am, don't resist!" Victoria had no intention of resisting. A great weariness came over her body, which quietly slumped into her adversary's arms. She was resigned and let him drag her to the exit, captive to a century that rejected her. The few remaining coins in her pocket jingled like a jailer's keys.

She picked out a colourful street, a clean staircase, a lively corner. If she must stay outside it might as well be a spot where she could enjoy the warmth of the people going by and the vibrant wave of the blue and purple storefronts. She parked herself on a squeaky step and watched the parade of humans, these creatures that, ultimately, she didn't understand at all. How had everything that was so easy in the twenty-fifth century become so hard? Maybe something had broken while she was travelling back in time, and the subtle organ that enables you to engage with others had been altered. Or maybe she had always been out of step with her fellows.

She jumped when the first coin clinked at her feet. Looking up, she saw a woman in a fur coat moving away. Had it dropped out of her purse? Victoria picked up the round dollar piece and stared at it. But before she could decide what to do with it, another passerby slipped her some small change. Victoria contemplated the coins that, to her astonishment, glinted in the palm of her hand. She'd been given alms.

All afternoon the money piled up in the pockets of Victoria's multiple articles of clothing. With each offering, she harked back to her twenty-fifth century penthouse, her jewellery, and the valuable paintings on the walls, which could have kept her afloat for years. Around three o'clock, a young man whose hair was done up in a mass of slender braids handed her a coffee, which she drank with pleasure. She then used the empty cup to collect donations. She received cigarettes, bread crusts, salted peanuts, and one man offered her a laughable sum in exchange for a blow job. Too stunned to speak, she slowly shook her head, no.

In the evening, she glided into a grocery store with the forty dollars she had amassed. She foraged in the aisles for the tastiest, warmest food, things that would melt and swell in her stomach and keep her whole. While she waited in line at the cash, her eyes fell on the cover of a magazine. In addition to an article revealing the secret of slimmer hips and ten tips for a zero-calories holiday season, it promised the list of the most beautiful women of 1999.

Victoria flipped through the periodical. Translucent skins, pumped-up eyelids, hollow chests, lips in a crimson pucker. Sullen silhouettes, melted stomachs, disciplined knees. Victoria perused the photos one at a time and then closed her eyes. It was all very clear. She replaced the magazine, which left her fingers redolent of ink and cheap perfume, paid for her purchase, and went out feeling that somewhere inside her a mainsail had just billowed out.

Immediately the next day she went back to the office of *La Perle* and dictated a second message to the clerk: *I AM UGLY HERE. RETURN IMPOSSIBLE. VICTORIA*. The man looked at her askance as she laid down her last coins to pay for the ad. Lighter now, she went back to her staircase and her paper cup. That night, a woman in tears stopped next to Victoria, wrenched a sparkling ring off her third finger, handed it to Victoria, and dashed away. Victoria gingerly tucked the jewel into her inside pocket. The idea of selling the wedding ring never crossed her mind.

The cold weather began to bite. Victoria kept warm with bland herbal teas and a moth-eaten parka given to her by an elderly couple. She fell into a routine like a stray cat in a deserted house. She awoke, filled up on dry croissants from the trash of a bakery, and then sat down at her usual spot to cadge for money. She lunched on broth and killed time in the afternoon when things were slow by talking to passersby who stopped to chat out of curiosity, kindness, or self-interest. In this city, homeless people served as confessional, lost-and-found, prey, or poem. Victoria adapted to all these functions.

At night, she slunk to the far end of an alleyway or under the deck of a café and wrapped herself in old newspapers. She promptly drifted off, caught in the net of her numbness and released into the warm seas of sleep. Had she glanced at the papers that she used as a blanket she might have seen this recurring message: *EON SEEKS VICTORIA TO FACILITATE RETURN. SIGNAL YOUR LOCATION*. But the troubled waters of night grew thicker, and Victoria no longer had any expectations.

The imminence of the new millennium was palpable everywhere: above the rooftops, in the graffiti, on signs displaying warnings and impossible wishes. The world seemed ready to tip over. This effervescence left Victoria breathless, and she sought refuge in the crevices where neither the oracles nor the merchants of the apocalypse could get in. She discovered that the beauty of Montreal lay less in its facades than its back streets, which brought you closer to the core, to the magma that was the organism's lifeblood.

Soon, however, no matter where she went, a reiteration loomed up in the landscape. At first it was just an impression, a familiar shadow that persisted like a floater. Little by little, her vision grew sharper and focused on the point of origin of this strange déjà vu. It was a man. He wore a ridiculous hat, like a bundle of fur apparently meant to stave off the assaults of incipient winter. Wherever she went, there he was, although he never seemed to follow her when she was on the move. He stared at her insistently, a look that she was not used to anymore. She sensed it in every breath he took, in his stubborn immobility—he wanted her. He wanted her with that dangerous desire, a desire that bides its time, that patiently mounts to the brink of the intolerable, that weighs on its object as it waits for a gesture to release it, to be unloosed. He watched her, and she realized she was going to die.

Victoria gave up her staircase, her alley, the greasy spoon where she gulped down her daily soup, and moved away from her usual territory, but he kept popping up, as if he had leapfrogged ahead of her. The next moment, he would vanish without a trace. She frantically moved from place to place, convinced that she could shake him off if only she found the right spot, some vast space charged with electricity, with the energy she had always lacked. A battleground where she could resist and hold up her refusal like a shield. The cold slashed at her bones, her nerves, and she strived with her whole body to turn that pain into a weapon. She had abandoned for good the neutral zones and friendly feelings. Perhaps her suffering would spawn a form of courage.

He was not there when she stumbled on the eight letters V-I-C-T-O-R-I-A carved into the pediment of a building. She was shivering when she halted in front of the hospital that looked like a castle. She approached the magnificent stone walls that protected a thousand lives, a thousand illnesses. The mountain rose up glowing against the night. Suddenly full of confidence, she skirted around the buildings and climbed up to the promontory where the city centre spread out before her. A match was about to end in a stadium below and the numbed November air was filled with the fans' triumphant shouts. The sensation of having conquered something welled up inside her. Without warning, a howl burst out of her, as if it had always been there, crouching in her gut, waiting for the moment when it would erupt and overpower every other sound nearby.

When she stopped and there was silence again, he was there. She hardly needed to turn around to see him standing behind her straight as a ramrod. Now the place from which her cry had sprung burned as though a sword had been thrust down her throat. This time, he didn't disappear.

As she slowly made her way into the woods, she guessed he was following her but keeping his distance so as not to scare her away before he pounced. She looked up at the moon swelling over the cold, apple-scented landscape. Soon she would have to fight. A wire fence appeared. She sensed her pursuer stopping, his heels sinking into the mud, his vile headgear bending the dry branches. "Are you Victoria?" The words drifted to her but she could not be sure he had actually said them. She was rooted to the spot, riveted to the fence that seemed to protect a treasure or a bottomless mine. The man's breath expanded and filled the woods, and Victoria felt the invisible sword plunge deeper into her throat.

Then, as if an extraneous finger had come to lift up her words and fling them into the air, she answered: "Yes, I am." And in a flash, she jumped. A prodigious bound that propelled her to the top of the barrier and over to the other side, where she landed gracefully. She was inexplicably certain he would not follow her into this enclosure. She had gone into another world.

At her feet, glimmering under the stars, was a swimming pool. Three-quarters full, covered with a crystalline layer of ice, the pool gently chewed on the mixture of mud and dead leaves floating in its water. Victoria watched the liquid swim around, much as countless patients undoubtedly had done in an effort to recover their strength. She took a deep breath. There might have been wolves, a mob, an execution squad on the other side of the fence. She was beyond their reach.

One effortless leap and she was in the water. Her dive broke the thin layer of ice and churned up the stagnant mire in the pool. The absolute cold of the pool engulfed all the others, the frostbite, the shivers, the cramps that had built up in her. At the bottom, everything became clearer, closer. She travelled back along a centuries-long thread. As she sank down, breathing in a liquid that at last restored her peace of mind, she evaded not just her pursuer but an entire epoch.

Weightless, her limbs stirred, opened up and dilated; her skin radiated a hazy luminescence under the shattered ice.

Her beauty, a new version of her beauty, regained possession of her exhausted body, and somewhere a perplexed man and a worried owl gathered fragments of it before she disappeared from view. Victoria had never been so beautiful, so invisible. She was as round as the invention of the wheel, as a rudder or a flooded hull. She was on her way home.

Victoria Down

PROSTRATE. THE WORLD COMES to her differently. The earth's belly is almost audible. Other sounds are dampened. She intones melodies, incantations, but there's nothing left but a thread of air. With no one to hear her, her voice has gone quiet.

She's been stretched out in this thicket for so long she thought she was turning into a snake, a lizard, or a salamander. Her legs are sunk in the ground, and she breathes with the worms. Mosses tried to grow on her back but couldn't gain a purchase there. She's as smooth as a stone pulled from a fire.

Before her eyes, the huts cave in and dissolve. Victoria never would have believed that what they'd built would crumble so quickly after they died. She hadn't realized how brittle their world was, barely sustained by the daily efforts of the people who made up her family. She'd like to get up and preserve these last buildings. She stays horizontal.

At times she sleeps, never for long. She dreams that others have survived and the survivors are standing up and walking toward her. Elated, she tries to open her arms to them, to talk to them, but she's unable. Her voice falls silent and her words collapse before crossing her lips.

Otherwise, she dreams of her own end. She sees herself lying flat in a muddy grave. Then she comes back to life, gets to her feet, and sinks back into death before rising once more and lying down again. This cycle repeats itself twelve times until she awakes.

In a panic, she tries to utter a sentence, a prayer. This is hard when you're voiceless. She's forgotten the most important words. Child. Fire. House. Her mother tongue, in which the first person was always plural and *people* and *family* were just one word, was intimately linked to the tribe. With the tribe gone, the words go missing.

There are also memories that can't be suppressed. The rumbling on the far side of the mountain. The arrival of the giants, with their snake-coloured costumes. Their eyes at once blue and green. The clubs in their hands and the blood they could spill with such monstrous ease. Their pointed phalluses, their ferocity toward the sisters and daughters, the mothers, even the elders. Death in a rolling boil of blood, piss, and shit.

She saw her people grab their little weapons designed to take down animals on the fly. She saw the strongest ones rise up to protect the others, the best warriors, the first to fall, without a fight, without honour. It came down to the little children, wielding spears, all of them filled with blinding bravery. All of them dead an hour later.

That is what she witnessed from the thicket where she still lies. Alarmed by the first detonations, she had dived for cover, face down. The giants caroused all through the night and left at dawn, when they'd had their fill. Victoria hasn't budged since that day. If she did get up it would be to take hold of an arrowhead and gouge out her eyes, slash her belly emptied of the children she had borne and let die, lacerate her genitals, which had loved the men who had fallen before her eyes without a sound. Voiceless.

Her throat is burning. Her chest wheezes. She opens her mouth wide to gather in the wind, hoping that the pollen drifting in the glade might soothe her. The flowers have opened and are sending out their call by the thousands through the dense forest. She finds their persistence somehow comforting. Animals race by without fearing her presence. She no longer has a scent. The village no longer has a scent. It's no longer a village.

Their prayers, tools, legends, hunts, lullabies, jewellery, trails, ovens, sacrifices, remedies—Victoria isn't able to latch on to anything anymore. Except herself, her posture of defeat in which there may possibly reside, if not a kind of courage then a form of resistance. So long as she is alive, they have not completely disappeared. Her cowardice then becomes a victory, her survival a celebration. She celebrates face down, her mouth in the earth.

The rain returns, lingers, and her body sinks into the mud. A little pond forms around her. Now she is half submerged and must raise her head to avoid swallowing water. But she doesn't leave her lair. The sound of the drops hypnotizes her.

Is she alive or dead? Is all of this just a dream; this clan that occupied the centre of the universe, had it really existed? If she expires, here, stretched out in the mud, if she dies with no one to bury her, to pray for her soul to cross the final rivers, if she disappears without anyone even noticing, will she have lived?

To drive away her doubts she clutches at a memory, grasps it tightly, and forces it to unfold day after day, hour after hour. A stormy night, gathered together in the great hut with herbal teas to keep warm and songs for protection. Babies nestled in the arms of children, children snuggled against the old folks. Nervous laughter between the rumblings of the sky. You had to stay together, resist the evil spirits with wakefulness. At last, a moonbeam shone down to announce the end of chaos, and sleep took everyone by surprise. Each one's breath, weight, sweat all jumbled together, they slept. She seizes this moment. She holds it.

Her teeth have fallen out. The earth instantly swallowed them up. She feels no pain, but something is missing. Night falls and falls again, fear returns. The shores move closer. Who knows which giants are preparing to march again, to cross the mountain, to hold back the dawn . . . She'd like to invoke the spirits of the elders, but she fears their forgiveness as much as their wrath.

The real battle begins the day the water completely covers her body. When this happens, Victoria isn't afraid anymore. Now there are only two possibilities. Either she gets up, walks over to the fruit tree, eats, dries herself off, regains her strength, builds a shelter, sleeps, fishes, lights a fire, maintains the light. Or she sinks deeper beneath this bush, in this ditch dug by her inertia. Her breathing slows, her voice recedes even more. Her limbs no longer obey. She has unlearned everything.

At the last moment, rage grabs hold of her, makes her blood surge and her lungs spew out the water inside them. She spits. She wants to get to her feet and race through the forest, climb the mountain, run until she meets a man, an eagle, or a puma that she can mate with and give birth to sons that she can mate with too, she wants to recreate her race from the little that's left of her. Her fury is such that she could take wing, plunge into the river, grapple with reptiles barehanded; she wants to shoot arrows into the northern sky, as many as it takes to make the rain stop and bring back the sun.

Has she stood up? Did she shout? What word did she hurl through the downpour, and where did it come down? The night's dark hands tighten around her throat. She never existed.

HEAVY JOWLS, bushy eyebrows, doleful eyes, and a receding chin. You'd think this woman was a baker or a janitor welded to her mop, spreading an odour of detergent and mould in her wake. A surly commoner who accidentally fell into the wardrobe of a regent. And yet, Germain muses as he continues to stare at the portrait displayed by his daughter, this really is the woman who held the reins of an empire, even giving her name to an entire era.

Are they making the same mistake with his Victoria? It was inferred from her tired bones and the sad features attributed to her that she had ended up alone because she had made a mess of her life. But this face, like the queen's, may be misleading, a mask hiding a heroic life. An unfinished, renewed, undying Victorian age. Germain, his eyes still fixed on the sovereign's portrait, squints in an attempt to animate her features, to make them smile, frown, and then open up, divulge their secrets, their pains and desires. Everything trapped under the appearance of immutability.

Shaking himself out of his daydream, he comes back to Clara rehearsing her oral presentation. Curled up inside herself, she seems to inhabit only a tiny corner of her body.

"Victoria reigned over the United Kingdom for more than sixty-three years. Her name has been used to describe the strict morality of that period. Many cities have been named in her honour, including the capital of British Columbia. Closer to home, the Victoria Bridge, built in 1860, was inaugurated by the queen's son Edward. At the time, it was considered the eighth wonder of the world. In Quebec City, the statue of Victoria was decapitated by the FLQ in 1963. Finally, Montreal's Royal Victoria Hospital has cared for the ill since 1893. That is where I was born, and that is where my father works. Victoria is all around us. She has become an integral part of our daily lives. For me, this is true celebrity. It is when your name becomes something greater than yourself."

She gives a comical bow. Germain applauds, congratulates her, but checks the urge to hug her. Without her imaginary audience, Clara becomes Clara again, her energy exploding in every direction and her body, which has grown too fast, contorting with every step. She goes upstairs, leaving Germain alone with the Queen's portrait, which she plans to take along for her talk on the topic of fame. Oral presentations are absolute torture for her. She clings to the little picture as if she could hide behind it.

In her bedroom, the half-light has transformed the colour of the walls, the texture of the carpet. The sun has almost disappeared behind the mountain. Clara glides over to the window seat and contemplates the silhouette of Mount Royal, the purple clouds dissolving around it. She likes to sit in this spot and study the landscape as if seeing it for the first time. To identify the turrets of the Royal Victoria, where she imagines her father's days, the difficulties and the triumphs that are basic to his work as a nurse. She thinks of the beginning of her own life in that stormy fortress overlooking the city. The smoke drifting up from the hospital brings to mind a fire smouldering under the roofs.

As a small child, she was certain that Mount Royal was a volcano. This legend, passed on from generation to generation in every Montreal schoolyard, was based mainly on the presence of a lake at the top of the mountain, a lake that was said to coincide with the crater's location. This belief kept Clara in a state of exquisite terror, the feeling that at any moment something huge, extraordinary, and tragic could take place. The volcano functioned as the monster under the bed, the bogeyman, but also as the enchanted castle, the imaginary friend. The horror stories she told hidden under a blanket to her cousins ended with a great BOOM, a spectacular eruption that wiped out everything.

When she learned that the lake, Beaver Lake, was actually an artificial pond, and the mountain no more than the wooded hill it appeared to be, she felt reassured. There was nothing for her father, her friends, and her to be afraid of anymore, neither the incandescent fingers of magma, nor the deadly volcanic vapours. But over the weeks, a strange impression crept into her mind. Instead of fear, she discovered a sort of lack. The great boiling heart that she had ascribed to Mount Royal was gone. Like a child who finds out that Santa Claus is a myth, Clara was deprived of something important. Her world had been planed down.

So she secretly began to believe in the volcano again. Encouraged by her readings about how the hill had come to be, she persuaded herself that the magma that had gone into its formation millions of years ago was still there, lurking so deep under the layers of rock that no one, not even the most eminent scientists, had detected it. She then convinced herself that the mountain was just the tip of the iceberg and the entire island of Montreal was a volcano that, sooner or later, would disfigure the map of the world. Now, every step she takes on the sidewalk manifests a kind of occult courage. Every day that goes by without a calamity is received as a happy reprieve. And every rumble she hears contains a threat, a challenge. To stay, to approach, to climb the mountain, to crouch very close to the ground and breathe in its perils, its enigmas. To survive.

Victoria

ALL THE WOMEN in my family are called Victoria, including me. It's not my real name.

I was born in the great flood. The whole lower city, its fringes and underskirts, drenched; Notre-Dame Hospital, flooded; Saint-Luc Hospital, flooded. My mother had to walk north, up to the Royal Victoria, where her waters broke too.

I was born when the first sign came of the end of the world, and I did not cry. I opened my eyes and a shout of victory went up. I grew up quietly, refusing to take the breast, sleeping with one eye open, avidly savouring the caresses of the reprieve. I had teeth before everyone else.

Now I'm seven years old and standing ankle-deep in water. Seven years of reason, of resignation. I live surrounded by many brothers and sisters, too many to count. And none of this will prevent my already charted future: I will die alone on earth.

They call me Victoria the same way they say "my girl," "little one." "A woman." It doesn't matter. Soon there will be no one left to utter my name.

At the hour of my death, I won't try to speak. I'll have nothing to say about the world, about what I learned here. I do my best not to draw lessons, not to become wiser. I want to have nothing to pass on.

When the time comes I won't struggle. There will be trees that are too young and a leaf-covered ground, nothing grand, nothing solemn. I'll be calm and silent. I'll be a grave that can't hold down what doesn't die.

I'm called Victoria, but that's not my real name. Because every name they give me is wrong. I have all the names of the world, the words of everyone who lived before me. I'm called mystery, pain, sometimes verdict. I'm an axe, a bomb armed and loaded, an arrow pointed at the last words of the story. I am courage, vestige, bridge. I am light.

I call myself victory, as in "the final." The last survivor. My name is love and war.

My name is eon. I'm an eternity, I'm everything, and then nothing.

Notes and Acknowledgements

BEHIND THESE PORTRAITS is a woman who actually existed. While my book is underpinned by the mystery surrounding her, I continue to hope that her true identity will eventually be discovered. Each chapter of *Madame Victoria* is entirely fictitious and intended as a tribute to this person, whose name is still unknown.

I am greatly indebted to the report aired on the ICI Radio-Canada Télé programme *Enquête*, which was the starting point of this project.

The poem sent by Hector in "Victoria in Love" borrows from Victor Hugo's "Je respire où tu palpites," which appears here in our translation.

The conversation between Loïc and the serial killer's wife is drawn from "The Truck Stop Killer," an article by Vanessa Veselka that appeared in the October 2012 issue of *GQ*.

As always, Antoine Tanguay's involvement was essential for the development of this book.

Thanks to Chloé Legault, Tania Massault, and Christine Eddie for their comments; to Dominique Fortier, my unsparing and indispensable editor; and to Sophie Marcotte for the final review.

Thank you, Alexandre, Catherine, Robert, Chantal, and Claude, my brave first readers.

Thank you, Sabrine Leblond-Murphy for clarifying the medical aspects of my stories, and for taking me on a fascinating tour of the labyrinthine Royal Victoria Hospital.

In 2015 the Royal Victoria Hospital closed, and a hospital of the same name was opened in a different location. No decision has been taken as yet concerning the fate of the old Royal Victoria Hospital buildings.

Thank you, Daniel Villeneuve, forever a son of Gagnonville, for his descriptions of the ghost city.

Finally, thanks to the members of my family, old and young, for understanding, respecting, encouraging, and reading.

About the Translator

LAZER LEDERHENDLER is a full-time literary translator specializing in Québécois fiction and non-fiction. His translations have earned awards and distinctions in Canada, the U.K., and the U.S.A. He has translated the works of noted authors including Gaétan Soucy, Nicolas Dickner, Edem Awumey, Perrine Leblanc, and Catherine Leroux. He lives in Montreal with the visual artist Pierrette Bouchard.